<u>The World of Present Future and Past</u>

<u>An adventure series</u>

Anita Kirk

Dedication

Anita's most popular fan would be
her father before he sadly got
dementia, and he is now
devastatingly blowing in the wind.
Anita's family has supported her
one hundred percent with her
writing, and she thanks them for
the encouragement and you for
taking the time out of your day to
pick her book up and read it.
If you do enjoy reading this book,
Anita would really appreciate a
good review to show other people
that you have enjoyed reading.

Acknowledgments

I would like to thank you for taking the time to pick this book out from the millions of books available out there to read, if you do enjoy reading this book your review would mean the world to Anita Kirk for her to enjoy reading and sharing this book with others on social media or in person would be most appreciated.

Thank you.

All characters and events in this book are fictitious, and any resemblance to real persons, living or dead, or to any event, past or present, is purely coincidental.

This book is for my mum

Prologue

There are two action-packed stories that follow each other in this book for all ages to enjoy.

A group of friends meet their future selves twice to save the world, with Charlie's dogs being the favourite of them all.

They tackle good magic and bad magic with dragons, mad magicians, rings, wizards, flying transport, strangers and so much more against them and some help them with magical tattoos that do so much.

They travel through time to different years and places.

They find themselves in sticky situations that can put them in danger.

Sleep is the key to winning items. You will never use a pen without looking at it strangely again after reading this book.

There are some funny moments inside that will keep you wanting more, keeping you entertained from start to finish.

Contents

Adventure One: In a Quarter of a Second

Adventure Two: The World of Present, Future and Past, The Glowing rings.

17: *They all picked a ring out of the envelope.*

18 *What do the oil, water and glass buttons do on the whistles?*

19: *Space bowlers looked at them, with them having different people with them.*

20: *They looked at the person they wished to swap their thoughts with.*

21: *Jake watched the ink appear back into the pen.*

22: *The undercover reflector-glass eyes disguise.*

23: *The tattoo bag had changed, from Bow to Jargin.*

24: *The virtual key on the outside of the bubble room.*

25: *The magical rings flashed pink.*

26: *The trees are being killed for dragon Vord on planet Opack.*

27: *George's memory jar had a blue smiley face that lit up. Then it popped open.*

28: *The fire started to chase them; it left smouldering marks on their clothes.*
29: *Robert removed the paper from the envelope in his pocket. Snowballs?*

The World of Present, Future and Past

Adventure One: In a Quarter of a Second

1

They looked at the strange whistles.

Charlie Pop explained. "I am fifteen years old, I have got two dogs that are the love of my life: Rex that is black, and Bruno, who is a chocolate, and cream colour, they are both dachshunds, they are stubborn, devoted, clever, lively, playful, and courageous, they have both got short legs, and long hair, they live with me and my parents, Kath goes out of her way to help if she can, with long blond wavy hair that is five feet six and Ronnie is six feet with short brown hair, and they have got a slim build."

It was dark outside with it being in the middle of the night, with him struggling to sleep.

Charlie carried on explaining. "Kath and Ron love to re-decorate their house and do any jobs that need doing when they are not space bowling."

It was the early hours of the morning.

"I am slim with short brown hair and I have got a pair of blue eyes that always sparkle with laughter, beneath brows that are a little bushy for me being so young, a red birthmark on the left side of my neck used to bother me when I was transitioning into my teens because I thought that it was ugly and it would turn the girls away, instead it seemed to be attracting them, like some kind of magic talisman that was making me irresistible and after falling in love six times during a two hours period, and one evening at the bowling club, it was more than my young heart could handle!"

The sky was starting to get lighter outside, with him hearing his mother outside of his door talking. "This smells so sweet!"

She was checking the wine in the airing cupboard, unable to sleep.

Charlie explained. "I was then thirteen, I was on an emotional roller coaster, with my brain in a place it had never been before, and thousands of gallant hormones who spent their entire existence training for the big moment were running wild!"

He slapped his forehead and groaned when he staggered out of the door feeling tired, walking over to his mother, with weakening knees and he almost swooned into her arms.

"Thank you, Mother ..." His voice was cracked and hoarse barely louder than a whisper, and he swallowed back on the lump in his throat before it choked him to death, his eyes were watering, and his soft Yorkshire accent became dreamier as he gripped her arms.

"You're the best Mother anyone could wish for!"

Ronnie joins them on the stairs, speaking. "I hope that none of you are drinking the wine yet, if you ever meet a lady friend, Charlie, she would love this sweet wine."

Charlie speaks. "I will meet someone one day, but not for a long time!"

Kath looks up at her husband, and the tone in her voice matched the astonishment on her face. "Eeee-what's gotten into your son, Ronnie Pop?"

His father shakes his head slowly, with a nonchalant expression, his voice as equally casual. "I dunno, Kath. I means, I know I was dumb at his age, but never as daft!"

Her eyes open wide and there is a sharp intake of air as her mouth drops open.

Ronnie shrugs. "What?"

"Oh, you lie, Mr Pops. I saw how you were with the McConnell twins when you walked past them!"

"You a thirteen-years old an' all, you should have known they were way out of your league and neither had the slightest interest in you."

"I only smiled back because they were smiling at me!"

Kath scoffs. "They were only smiling because you were staring at them goggle-eyed, with a stupid grin on your face, and they could see what you didn't."

"And' what was that?"

"The lamp post that you walked into."

Ronnie grunted and turned his eyes away with an embarrassed expression on his face. "So, you were watching me way back then, huh?"

"Ever since my father broke a full-length mirror in their bedroom, my mother got upset, because it would bring them seven years of bad luck, and I heard her yelling at him!"

'We could end up with Ronnie Pop as a son-in-law because of your carelessness.' So, I started watching you. I wanted to know why my mum was so worried!"

Charlie is resting his head on her left shoulder with his eyes closed, and a distant smile on his lips, he sighs and grips her arms tighter. "I just want to thank you for giving me this ... this thing on my neck, it's such a wonderful gift!"

Charlie walked back into his room and chilled out on his bed nodding off, after a few hours he woke up with the smell of paint, thinking that his dad was painting again on the stairs, thinking to himself that he had only painted the stairs six months before wondering what colour the walls would be this time, he was looking forward to talking to his space bowling friends on a face time group chat when he had got dressed to discuss the space bowling game in his large bedroom that has got a large wardrobe, a dressing table with a chair at the side of his double bed, and cream coloured walls.

They were going to play soon together against the Bay Boot team, him and his bowling friends, they had been going to the Landfawcett space bowling centre all of their lives, with their parents playing knocking the swiper cones down.

It was their space bowling tournament that day, Charlie's dad was still re-decorating the staircase outside of his bedroom, with him opening his bedroom door noticing that he was painting the walls, from light yellow to cream stopping Rex and Bruno from leaving his room onto the steps, noticing the paint tray on the floor in front of his bedroom door saying good morning to his father, with him saying, good morning back.

Charlie walked out of his room to get a shower in the bathroom opposite his room, at the top of the stairs as he walked out of the bathroom, he stepped over the paint tray walking back into his room, with a large white towel around him shutting his door again.

Charlie face-timed his friends sitting in his towel on his phone, discussing the space bowling game that they were going to play, swiper alley, having a go at knocking ten swiper cones down discussing what they were doing after the game.

Charlie mentioned to his father, and through the camera to his friends, that he was going for a drink downstairs, leaving his bedroom door open.

Charlie's father (Ronnie) said loudly. "Look what has happened!

Rex and Bruno have stepped into the paint, and jumped onto your chair, then onto your bed."

Kath heard what was going on walking upstairs in a fast, abrupt, and angry manner behind Charlie, saying that she was not incredibly happy with Charlie, and asked him why he did not shut his room door.

Furiously, Charlie's Mum Kath stormed into the room as she explained that she had only just cleaned the bed sheets.

Ron was still grumbling that he was up the stepladder and that he had no chance of stopping the dogs from stepping into the paint.

Charlie helped to change the bed sheets with, Kath, and cleaned the room the best that they could using paint remover as required that smelt disgusting, as she calmed down, Kath explained to Charlie that Rex and Bruno should have been on leads, opening the window to let the strong smell out, then went to fetch something.

Kath gave him a handful of whistles for him, his friends, and Rex and Bruno to enjoy, explaining that a brightly dressed man who had a bright yellow suit with an orange tie, and blue shoes in the market that she had never met before had given her the whistles, saying that they were lucky charms for, Charlie, and his friends.

Charlie showed the whistles to everybody over his computer on face time, with them wondering why they had been given the lucky charms.

Charlie's friends looked close up at the computer screen to look as closely as they could.

Charlie explained." There is a yellow string to hang around our necks;

the whistle is a similar size, and shape to a small blue phone!"

Chris pointed out the on and off buttons at the side of the blue talk button, with talk holes around the whistle, and an orange button saying skates on it.

Darren pointed out the camera, saying. "I wonder if it works?"

Eric noticed and pointed out a black small smooth shiny stone button.

Robert could not understand the yellow button with no writing.

Jay looked puzzled at the tiny black dial at the side of the whistle, above the dial, there was writing saying forward and back, with small numbers on a screen covered in see-through plastic, with the numbers two-thousand and twenty-five written on the whistle.

Tom pointed out the compass next to the dial with it saying Landfawcett in the left corner, Bay Boot in the right corner, Magictastic in the bottom left, and Village Moto in the bottom right.

Harry noticed a clear raised button with amnesia written at the bottom of the whistle underneath, and a clear tiny, raised button light.

Charlie pulled a shower cap hat out of a tiny secret compartment, looking at it puzzled, then put it back.

George looked at his whistle oddly. "These whistles belong to a superhero, I think!"

They all agreed.

Robert grunted. "More like a kid's toy!"

Charlie's dad, Ron, walked in handing Charlie his yellow T-shirt with space bowling written on it, and his black trousers with him saying that he needed to go soon, as it was a ten minutes' walk from their house.

Charlie announced. "See you all at the Landfawcett space bowling, and ice-skating centre for our game!"

He then turned the computer off and picked the strings up with the whistles on the ends.

He walked out of the house eating a bacon sandwich in one hand, and Rex and Bruno, on a lead in his other hand, struggling to hold the whistles slightly as well.

Kath his mum gave Charlie some money and asked him to go to the shop on the way to get a print off of the lotto numbers to check the last draw on the nineteenth of April twenty-twenty-five and get a lucky dip lottery ticket at the same time for the next draw.

Charlie replied proudly. "Yes, I will now that I am fifteen years old, and I am now allowed to buy them!"

Charlie put the strings from the whistles on the floor, while he put the money into his wallet, putting his wallet back into his pocket, he then picked the whistles back up, and then he walked off slowly.

Kath and Ronnie spoke in sync with each other. "Thank you, see you later Charlie!"

Charlie shouted you're welcome back, then walked down in the warm sunshine to his space bowling game, with the whistles still in his hand tying Rex and Bruno up outside of the small, cluttered shop with him walking into Landfawcett stores asking for a lucky dip lotto ticket for the next draw, and a printout of the nineteenth of April twenty-twenty-five lotto numbers.

The lady handed the lottery ticket to Charlie, putting it onto the counter.

Charlie put the whistles onto the counter for a moment, then he put the lotto ticket and numbers into his wallet grumbling what a waste of money it was, because his mum never wins and removed the money from his wallet and handed the money over.

The lady commented. "I have never seen whistles like that before, where have they come from?"

Charlie had a disgusted look. "I think that somebody thinks that me and my bowling friends are younger than we are, they were a gift, but they look like they are for a five-year-old to play with!"

The lady replied. "Okay, check them out before you give them away!"

Charlie replied. "I will do!"

Charlie then waved goodbye to the shop lady, then untied Rex and Bruno, and carried on walking, arriving at the Landfawcett Space bowling centre and walked inside.

Charlie let Rex and Bruno walk around freely with him, handing the whistles to all of his friends.

The bowlers sat on brown stools, and comfy reclining red chairs with drinks and chatted amongst themselves.

Charlie bought a pint of lemonade joining everybody.

Charlie's friends are called, Harry Em who is six feet two with a high-pitched voice that could shatter glass, and he also has got a slim build.

Eric Tweet is very well-spoken, and he is four feet six, and very fit and toned from a lot of exercising, he is obsessed about wanting to kiss a girl one day and he is easily pleased and outgoing.

Paul Key is a shy person who finds it hard to talk to new people but thinks that he knows everything, he has got a hoop earring in his right ear.

Robert Storm is five feet two, he tries to always wear black with him being a goth, he is very sociable, and he has got a small key ring with a picture of his favourite game, the Landfawcett space bowling blue and yellow slim striped swiper cones that they knock down with a small orange ball when playing the game, with him being a little chubby, and he has got ginger hair.

Chris Leaf, is an emotional person that gets a little agitated easily, but he is always reliable and always does what he says he will do, and he is five feet three, and he has got blond short hair and a medium to large build.

Jay Laugh is always in a rush and loves to be in control of everything, he is a very likeable, and favourable person, and he is six feet seven.

Darren Rain is a very calm, confident person with shoulder black length hair and loves to share his things, he has got a kind and thoughtful heart, he is six feet four and would love to have a tattoo saying, bavarder, meaning chat in French because he can't keep his thoughts to himself and never stops talking.

Tom Breeze has got short hair, and he dresses casually with him always happy; he has got awards in swimming, and darts, and he has got a very toned up stomach, and he is muscular, and he is six feet six and has got a passion to win in everything.

Ben Steps and George Sing wear glasses and have awards for making the best comedian impressions, they keep the peace with people to keep everybody, and everything calm.

Jake Train is six feet one with dark brown short hair, he is the cleverest of them all, he has invented a secret waterproof wireless finger camera that takes photographs; it is attached to one of Charlie, and his friends' fingers.

Rex and Bruno have got a camera attached to their fur on their heads; images are shared with each other from the app recording onto their iPads, phones, and laptops.

Rex and Bruno looked happy with everybody fussing over them, the bowlers placed the whistles around their necks and put Rex and Bruno's whistles around their necks as well, they then finished their drinks.

Rex and Bruno stayed behind the bar with Lezley as normal while the team played space bowling.

The Bay Boot opposition team were losing, Harry felt elated because their team was winning.

Ben could not understand why the Bay Boot team was written on their whistles.

Robert was taking his turn bowling his ball down to the ten swiper cones, hoping that they would all go down.

Chris could not understand why Rex and Bruno had got a whistle.

Darren sounded concerned. "Maybe your mum should not have accepted the whistles, especially from a stranger!"

Alec in charge said happily. "You just have a few more strikes, then you have won!"

Jake looked hopeful. "Concentrate on the game, then we can win!"

In the end, the game was a draw.

Ben sighed. "It makes it fair and no bad feelings between each other, we will have another space bowling game another day soon, we can try to win next time!"

Harry suggested. "Maybe the whistles want us to be friends with the Bay Boot team?"

Alec congratulated both teams for doing really well in the space bowling game, they walked over to the Bay Boot team and had a drink with them in the reception bar.

Rex and Bruno ran up to everybody, wagging their tails and sitting on the floor at the side of them.

The other team looked at the whistles and asked what they were for.

Chris and Robert together started explaining about the strange man from the market.

Paul panicked because he could not take his whistle from around his neck to show everybody; the more he tried to remove the whistle, the more it tightened.

Everybody else's was the same, with them panicking a little.

Robert suggested. "Let's blow the whistles for fun to see what they sound like!"

Harry blew his whistle; it repeated the name Emily continually.

Bruno and Rex started barking at the noise.

George's whistle had a group of people singing. 'Welcome to Magictastic.'

Jake's sounded like rain.

Ben suggested. "I think that everybody should attempt to remove the whistles again after the train noise!"

They agreed that they were silly but fun, agreeing to give them to some children to play with, they struggled to try to take them off, trying not to strangle themselves.

Robert suggested. "Let's try to cut the whistles off with a pair of scissors!"

They tried to cut the string, but the scissors would not go anywhere near the string, there seemed to be a force field stopping the scissors from cutting it.

Harry and Jake both pressed most of the buttons on their whistles at the same time, with nothing happening.

Robert could not understand why the whistles were still stuck to them.

George suggested. "We need to put the whistle near to Rex and Bruno's mouths to see if they will make a noise!"

Bruno's whistle stayed in the air next to his mouth, with nothing holding it up for a few minutes, even though George had let go of it.

Bruno's whistle sounded like fireworks.

Eric put Rex's whistle into his mouth, and it sounded like somebody shaking a 'Bag of beads.'

Rex's whistle stayed near his mouth, the same as Bruno's.

"It is so weird." Harry said.

Jake pulled a face. "These whistles are rubbish and far too strange for me, let's all try harder to rip them off, then throw them away!"

Charlie looked at Rex and Bruno and wondered how he could remove them from the dogs without hurting them.

George was unable to take off Rex and Bruno's whistles, but accidentally knocked the dial, and the yellow button on his own whistle, the screen displayed a forward sign, and the numbers above showed two-thousand and fifty-five.

George disappeared.

Suddenly, they could all hear George's voice, but he had mysteriously vanished from sight.

Rex and Bruno started barking, obviously sensing that George was missing.

2

If we press, he may hear us.

Everybody started getting worried, wondering what had happened to George, with them starting to look for him, but there was no sign of him anywhere.

Paul suggested. "If everybody presses the blue talk button, George may be able to hear us!"

They all pressed their blue button.

Suddenly, George's voice came across through all of the whistles with his face on the camera.

George had a puzzled look. "Everybody has disappeared, but I am still sitting at the bar alone with no lights on, that is what it looks like to me, and it is now dark outside of the window!"

Tom said to George. "Find the raised light at the bottom of your whistle."

George explained. "I have found the light button, and I can see better now that I have turned it on!"

Charlie, Paul, and Harry all were saying, you are definitely not at the bar.

Darren, Paul, and Chris were replying as well, saying. "It is not dark outside here; it is sunny here with blue sky!"

George walked towards the wall, stumbling over chairs and tables to find the light switch and switched it on, explaining that he could see that it was definitely the same Landfawcett bar that he was sat in earlier; explaining that it looked a little different with some obscure pictures, with a picture of their team winning in two-thousand and fifty-five on the wall.

Paul suggested to George. "Why don't you turn your dial back to two-thousand and twenty-five and press your yellow button to see if you can be transported back to us?"

"Okay." George agreed with Paul.

All of a sudden, George appeared.

Robert suggested. "Now that we know we can all get back to the year two-thousand and twenty-five, let's all go and have a look at the year two-thousand and fifty-five!"

Eric questioned everyone. "Who is in favour of going to two-thousand and fifty-five, put your hand up, if yes!"

3

They all vanished.

Everybody voted, putting their hands up immediately saying see you later to the Bay Boot space bowling team.

The Bay Boot space bowlers laughed and asked where they were going.

Darren replied, smiling. "We are hopefully going on an adventure!"

Tom suggested for them to see if the camera on the whistle worked.

Charlie got everyone from his team, and the Bay Boot team together snapping a photo of them up close, struggling to get everybody in on the shot, with everyone else getting a photo shot of that photo taken as well on their whistles.

The bowlers said goodbye, turning their dials and pressed their yellow buttons.

Charlie and Tom pressed Rex and Bruno's dial to two-thousand and fifty-five and pressed their yellow buttons as well.

They started looking around the room, puzzled.

George questioned. "What do you think everybody now that I have turned the light on previously?"

Jay said. "It is a change, and hopefully, a bit of an adventure for us all, the dogs might find it a bit strange though!"

Darren looked to see if there were any batteries inside of the whistle, realising that there was no opening, he blew his whistle laughing because it sounded like heavy rain falling into puddles, and it connected with his surname.

Paul found a 3D Landfawcett Express newspaper lying on the table, he picked it up, and it displayed the twenty-second of April twenty-fifty-five, it was 3D, and everything in the paper looked as if it was real life happening in front of them.

Darren was shocked because he was on the front page looking older; it said that he was famous because he had created a Landfawcett smart flower which creates playing card animals that come to life with the smart flowers' magic, the clock on the wall showed two in the morning.

Jay randomly blew his whistle; it sounded like people laughing; he did not understand why the whistles were connected to their surnames.

Chris looked a little confused. "I wonder why all of our whistles are flashing blue?"

Jake suggested. "Maybe it means that something is about to happen?"

They all looked confused because the time had changed from two in the afternoon to two in the morning.

Rex and Bruno walked behind the bar looking for Lezley, but they could not find her, there were different bottles of alcoholic drinks behind the bar.

The bowlers decided to walk behind the bar with Rex and Bruno and helped themselves with Darren speaking. "What type of dogs live in Draculas castle?"

Jake quizzed. "I would like to know the answer!"

Darren answered. "Bloodhounds."

The bowlers laughed.

Darren gave Rex and Bruno food and drink.

The bowlers chatted about how good it was that they could drink while they were all under the legal drinking age.

Charlie blew his whistle; it sounded like a pop can opening.

Darren picked up a red and black bottle with a label saying Qui seven percent volume alcohol written on it saying. "What did the bartender say after a book walked in?"

Jake poured everybody a large glass full, they picked their glasses up to smell the no-aroma drink replying. "What is the answer?"

Darren replied. "Please, no stories."

Everybody laughed, agreeing that they were pleasantly surprised discussing how nice the sweet-tasting non-fizzy Qui was, with them drinking eight big bottles between them.

Chris poured a drink called Blue Rock Cool for everybody, including Rex and Bruno, and it had an orange and pink label with six percent volume of alcohol.

Jay asked Chris to blow his whistle.

Chris then blew his whistle, with him talking about how silly it sounded with a unique leaf crunching under your feet noise that was connected to his surname as well.

Rex and Bruno drank it fast, everybody drank nine bottles of the Blue Rock Cool between them, with them discussing how fruity and refreshing it tasted.

Tom picked up a small plastic one hundred orange and bronze coin from the floor, it had a picture of the man that had given Charlie's mum the whistles from the Landfawcett market, and it had writing that said the City of Magictastic on it, with the other side of the coin that had got Mad Magician written on it, a picture of a strange-looking animal with three tails, and the word Umbazan was written below the picture.

The bowlers had a discussion about the strange coin.

Robert looked very puzzled, wondering why the man in the market from the year two-thousand and twenty-five would be on the coin in the year two-thousand and fifty-five.

Tom announced. "I will put the coin into my pocket, I am just thinking, why should you never listen to coins?"

Robert replied. "I don't know?"

He then blew his whistle; it sounded like a thunderstorm.

Tom replied. "Because it never makes any cents!"

Paul laughed, setting everyone else off.

Tom, Paul, and Ben suggested going through to the ice rink area, everybody liked that idea apart from Jay who was worried that they might fall over because they were all a little drunk.

George sounded positive. "It will be fun!"

Everybody stumbled into where the ice skates were kept, putting ice skates on and wobbling onto the ice whilst chatting amongst each other.

Harry suggested in his high-pitched voice, saying that it would be great if there was a bit of music to listen to and have a dance and sing along.

Jay went into the staff area to put the radio on, the songs were different to the year two-thousand and twenty-five, but they still enjoyed them with them being funky and upbeat.

Robert suggested playing a game of space bowling down the ice, with the person who bowls the furthest down the ice wins.

Rex and Bruno ran straight around the corner onto the ice, sliding about on their paws a little tipsy.

The bowlers found this hilarious, looking funny at them, laughing at them so loudly.

George shouted. "Everybody follow me to collect the balls and swiper cones!"

They followed George.

Eric blew his whistle on the way; it sounded like a bird tweeting.

When they had got all of their items, they walked back to the ice rink and threw the balls as fast as possible down the ice one at a time hoping that each of their balls would go the furthest, it was funny the way their balls slid down the ice.

Everybody helped themselves to Qui at the ice bar.

Rex and Bruno lay at the side of the ice, watching them all drunk and wobbly.

Ben had won the game, and he blew his whistle to celebrate, which sounded like heavy footsteps.

Everybody shook his hand with praise and enthusiasm, hugging him, they had drunk too much, so they all sat down to rest on the seats at the side of the ice for a brief time.

Charlie suggested skate dancing speaking. "What did the ice cube say to the glass of water?"

Paul looked puzzled. "I don't know?"

Charlie answered." I am cooler than you."

They all laughed, agreeing on singing as well, they all picked up some loose ice and threw it at each other, starting an ice fight.

Harry went to turn the music down.

Paul decided that it would be an excellent idea to make their own song up and that it would be fun, looking even giddier announcing it to the rest of the space bowlers suggesting that whoever starts to sing, throws ice at the next person that they choose to sing.

Darren blew his whistle with Tom singing. "Puddles are made from rain, what an amazing time that you have jumping into puddles, the only downside is that you get wet!"

George blew his whistle with it singing. 'Welcome to Magictastic' as well, with the puddle sound in the background.

Darren stopped blowing his whistle with no more puddle noises.

Jake put Rex's button to his mouth, and Rex's whistle sounded like a bag of beads.

George threw ice at Darren.

Darren started singing. "Beads, and Magictastic what a strange combination, you both sound different, I wonder if you are both connected!"

Eric blew his whistle with a bird-tweeting noise.

George stopped blowing his whistle with the singing stopping.

Darren threw ice at George and Robert, laughing.

George started to sing. "Birds and beads, what a strange combination, that sounds like birds, and the Bees!"

Robert sang. "The Bees and birds buzz like a warmth of fresh honey!"

Robert threw ice at Jay, and George threw ice at Jake.

Paul blew his whistle with a jingling key noise, and Tom had removed Rex's whistle with the bead noise stopping.

Jay started singing. "Jingling and tweeting what a nice relaxing noise, how amazing and good is that!"

Jake sang. "I wish that the jingling was the key to my own front door with a bird in my garden, then you could all come over and have a party with me!"

Eric and Paul stopped blowing their whistles, with the tweeting and jingling noises stopping.

Jay threw ice at Charlie, and Jake threw ice at Harry.

Jay blew his whistle with a laughing noise.

Harry put Bruno's whistle up to his mouth, with a fireworks going off noise with lots of bangs.

Charlie sang. "I love bonfire night; it is so amazing and with other people laughing, it makes me feel happy and warm!"

Harry sang. "Fireworks how amazing, what is much better than this, people laughing is a sign that they are happy, and I love that!"

Charlie threw ice at Ben, and Harry threw ice at Eric.

Jay stopped blowing his whistle with the laughing noise stopping, and Robert took the whistle out of Bruno's mouth with the fireworks noise stopping.

Harry put his whistle into his mouth with it saying Emily on repeat, and Chris putting his whistle into his mouth, with a crunching under your feet noise, and Robert put his in as well with a thunderstorm noise.

Ben sang. "What goes up when the rain comes down, and thunderstorms, I hate the noises with the wind howling the most, but I love the sound of leaves crunching under your feet, and who is Emily?"

Harry sang. "I would love to know the answer and Emily may be my true love one day, I hope as I love the name, I could walk through the park in a thunderstorm with her holding her hand so that we can calm each other, if and when I meet her one day!"

Ben replied. "An umbrella goes up, of course, as it starts to rain!"

They stopped blowing their whistles with the leaf, and the

thunderstorm and Emily on repeat noises stopped.

Ben laughed, throwing ice at Chris, and Eric threw ice at Paul.

Ben blew his whistle with a heavy footsteps noise.

Tom blew his whistle with a strong breeze noise.

Jake blew his whistle with it sounding like a train, and Charlie started to blow his whistle with it sounding like a pop can opening.

Chris started to sing. "The heavy footsteps and the strong breeze sounds a little frightening, but a nice cosy warm train would pick us up to make us feel comfy and warm with a can of pop to chill out with us at the side of us!"

Paul ended the music with. "Trains help you along the way to get you from A to B with you walking the rest of the way with a can of pop, and a strong breeze pushing you along the way!"

They put their whistles away, with the noises stopping.

Robert mentioned. "I am just going for a walk around to try to dry off and remove my skates, you carry on!"

After a while, everybody removed their skates.

Robert walked back towards them as he had discovered a note on the reception door stating that the space bowling and ice-skating centre was closed tomorrow twenty-third of April.

"Brilliant!" everybody excitedly said.

They were happy to have longer to drink more alcohol, and they all walked to the reception bar with Rex and Bruno.

Chris and Jay went into the kitchen to make pie and chips.

Jay rushed over in a rush as usual to turn the music off to give them a rest.

Everybody then walked into the kitchen one at a time to collect their food.

Rex and Bruno got plenty of attention.

Tom blew his whistle because he liked the sound of the strong breeze noise.

Ben said how tired they all looked as it was nine-thirty in the morning, and they had been drinking all night, they settled down and slept in the bar.

They all woke up at five in the afternoon and ate cereal.

Paul blew his whistle to wake them up properly, with it sounding like keys jingling, he decided that it was really super strange, and odd, that all of the whistles were connected to their surnames.

The bowlers decided to look for a key so that they could go outside looking high and low, finding the key behind a crisp box and unlocked the door, stepping outside, they could hear loud weird noises coming from across the road.

George had never seen such a long queue of people blowing whistles or heard anything like it before as the whistle noises were so loud.

4

They investigated the noises.

They walked over the road to find out why people were blowing their whistles.

George held Rex and Bruno on their leads.

Robert and Darren commented that they could hear the sound of a train above them, the same as Jake's whistle sounds when blown.

Robert looked up. "It looks like there are some rails hovering in the sky!"

People were floating up to a floating platform at the side of the rails in the sky, it seemed impossible because there was no solid structure to hold the rails up, the sun was shining so it was hard to see above them, they got in the queue to see what these people were queuing for, noticing that people had a small round bar code tattoo on the top of their hand, some said Magictastic, some said Bay Boot and some said Landfawcett, the bowlers all commented on how strange the tattoos looked.

Darren said jokingly. "If we all press the black button and blow our whistles at the same time, we can see what happens!"

Darren placed Rex's whistle up to his mouth, and put his finger onto Rex's button, while Charlie placed Bruno's whistle to his mouth and got ready to press his button, they put their whistles in their mouths and blew together, and everybody counted down 'three, two, and one' then pressed the black smooth button and blew their whistles simultaneously.

Rex and Bruno just breathed or barked, and that was their way of blowing their whistles, everybody floated up into the air, and a girl appeared on the hovering platform in front of them.

Charlie asked the girl's name, with her replying. "My name is Emily!"

Charlie replied. "That is strange, my whistle says your name on repeat, and my surname is Em!"

"Maybe this is meant to be!" Harry announced.

Emily replied sternly. "Maybe, you need to take your fingers off the black button and stop blowing your whistles continually to stop floating upwards, then give one short blow to stop yourselves completely floating up, and then you will be able to hover at the side, then onto the transparent platform!"

Paul replied. "We have stopped floating up, it sounds so loud, please grab us as we float towards you!"

Charlie replied. "Now that everybody is on the platform, I have tied Rex and Bruno to the metal bar to stop them from falling off!"

Charlie asked Emily where the whistles had come from, and why people have them.

Emily replied. "It is how we live with dissimilar kinds of magic from the whistles doing different things when blown, and separate buttons are pressed to help in different situations!"

The bowlers looked at each other.

Emily thought that Charlie looked familiar, he reminded her of a boy named Charlie that is older than him, with two dogs that he had with him regularly until they had died.

Charlie looked puzzled after Emily had said that.

Emily spoke. "Do you want me to organise your journey, where are you destined on the sky train?"

Jay replied in a confused tone of voice. "We don't know why we are here, or where we are going, can you suggest a good place?"

Emily replied. "I suggest that you go to Magictastic, the sky train is due in the next ten minutes, so go and sit down on the comfy blue chairs, there is a water fountain if you need a drink!"

Robert replied. "That sounds good!"

Emily explained. "A person called Darren who looks a spitting image of you, he has invented the smart flower, and it helps to protect me, and not many others from evil in a small village which is called Moto, he uses special soil from certain protected parts, and it has worked for years, the soil homes this extraordinary white, smart flower which also creates a powerful force field around anybody entitled to it!"

5

Maybe you are here for a reason.

Darren had a Cheshire grin on his face and thought that maybe this was his future self that had invented this magic smart flower which protected them from wicked evil powers.

Everybody discussed how strange it was that a flower could do these things.

Emily explained. "I also use my 3D map, it has got very clear details of roads, paths etc that we can follow like we are in the map that Wizard Moto has invented, with details of where all the sky platforms are, and where all of the sky rails travel to, and also the details of the ground below!"

Chris asked. "Why is Magictastic written on the whistles?"

Emily replied. "Maybe you are all here for a reason to help the city of Magictastic and the people that live there!"

Charlie replied. "It sounds too unreal to me, Magictastic there is no such place!"

Emily disagreed. "Magictastic does exist, they need help, so I have heard from the city people that get onto the sky rail, the Mad Magician was good, and he has turned to evil!"

Jake replied, not wanting to know. "We hope that somebody helps the Magictastic city people!"

Jay replied. "I hope the Mad Magician isn't that bad, what on earth is he doing to the people of Magictastic?"

Emily spoke. "The Mad Magician listens to peoples' conversations through his whistle sometimes, he makes life hard by letting his pet dragon Umbazan out of his cage to take away important items that make electricity for the city of Magictastic!"

Robert and Paul said together. "That does not sound good!"

Emily replied. "It is not good at all, you normally know when the Mad Magician is going to cause mischief, there is a strong blue light from his whistle, it points up to the sky which you can see from wherever you are in the country!"

Ben replied. "It is strange how the Mad Magicians whistle can be so bright!"

Emily replied. "Umbazan has got three strong long tails, they wag that hard on the ground it shakes because they are that big and powerful, a giant head with big brown eyes, a tiny nose, a large mouth with big sharp white teeth, a large plain shaped body with dark brown fur, four legs, large paws, and long sharp nails that would tear you apart!"

Darren replied. "I would not like to be in Umbazan's path, it sounds like they are both very scary and dangerous!"

Emily commented. "If Umbazan comes near you in charge mode, run away fast, or he will crush anybody or anything that he goes near!"

Harry commented. "Umbazan is not like most people, some people don't move to do work unless you set their bottoms on fire with a rocket, Umbazan is out of control!"

Emily carried on explaining. "You are funny, Umbazan, and the Mad Magician has got good and bad powers, the Mad Magician tells Umbazan where to go to find people to hurt or kill them!"

Rex and Bruno looked tired.

Emily said that she had never heard of two-thousand and twenty-five asking if it was a new place that she could look up to retrieve information about their destination.

Charlie explained. "Two-thousand and twenty-five is the year that we have all come from, and we will travel back through the whistles when we have explored everything!"

6

They got ready to float down.

Robert questioned Emily with a puzzled look. "How does the sky platform stay floating in the sky with no supports?"

Emily answered. "It was the Mad Magician's good magic that keeps it up in the sky before he turned nasty, everybody likes using the sky platform, it makes it safer when getting on and off the sky rail!"

Tom commented on untying Rex and Bruno. "It would be nice to be back with my family, and friends in two-thousand and twenty-five for my birthday tomorrow!"

Emily beamed glowingly. "Happy birthday for tomorrow, Tom!"

Tom smiled. "Thank you!"

Robert changed the subject, suggesting that they should go down to the ground.

George put the whistles into Rex, and Bruno's mouths, and put his finger onto Rex's orange button so that Rex was ready.

Harry put his finger on Bruno's orange button on his whistle.

Robert counted down three, two, and one, everybody pressed their orange button, then blew their whistles together, and everybody stepped off the platform shaking and feeling scared in case they fell to their death, they then floated down, and roller skates appeared on everybody's feet, including Rex and Bruno's paws.

Emily shouted. "The reason that everybody's shoes and paws had turned into roller skates is because you pressed the orange button to change back to shoes, just press the orange button again, and I might see you later!"

Jake and Paul shouted to Emily. "Okay, we understand, bye for now!"

Eric replied. "Do you know why my crazy mum put roller skates on her rocking chair?"

Jay answered. "Why did she do that?"

Eric replied. "Because she wanted to rock and roll."

Robert replied. "I like that, I am pleased that we have all reached the ground safely!"

They were so pleased to be back on the ground they started to pretend to kiss the ground, laughing and feeling incredibly happy.

Eric sounded dreamy. "I just wish that I could kiss a sexy girl!"

Robert replied to Eric. "One day hopefully we all will kiss a girl; we are all in the same boat and have never kissed a girl before!"

Tom, Jay, and George discussed together, suggesting that it would be a good idea to skate to older Charlie's house, discussing while travelling that they hope that they did not get locked up, because older Charlie phones the police, or thinks that he is going crazy, with him thinking that he was seeing things, with him seeing them all and his younger self.

They happily agreed setting off.

On the way, they noticed the scenery had changed now that they were in two-thousand and fifty-five discussing all of the changes below.

They finally arrived at Charlie's house; it had changed from what it normally looked like, in the driveway, there were two strange purple cars with small wings on either side of the cars, the cars looked as if they could fly, as they approached the front door it became clear that the front door was open.

Harry said to Charlie. "I dare you to go inside!"

Charlie pushed the front door open, noticing the same layout as two-thousand and twenty-five.

"Get out of my house!" A voice shouted.

A man was standing in the hall, and Charlie could see that it was himself thirty years older probably, he shivered, it was such a shock to see himself older trying to explain to his older self that he had been transported from the past by the whistles.

The man would not listen to him and shouted. "Don't be daft, there is no way that you have come from the past, stop messing about and get out of my house before I call the police!"

Older Charlie started to calm down, and he started to look at younger Charlie and his friends.

He had a photograph of the space bowling team on his hall table which looked exactly like all of the people standing in front of him, how could this be possible, he thought, with a puzzled expression on his face.

Darren commented. "I am just glad that you are starting to believe us all!"

Older Charlie started to listen to what Charlie was saying and wondered if it could be all true, and decided to let them stay offering them some food and a drink, he wanted to know more about these strange people, and couldn't believe that this was his younger self looking at the photograph again still in shock with it looking like all of them.

Younger Charlie mentioned how strange it was that the photo that he was holding was taken the day before, but it was years old.

Robert spoke. "Thank you for believing us!"

Older Charlie excitedly said that he would ring his space bowling friends to see if they could come over, he had decided that he would not tell his friends why until they had arrived.

Charlie and his friends discussed that they would like to see their older selves, with them deciding that it would be an excellent idea to stay in the kitchen to wait until everybody had arrived.

7

They could not believe their eyes.

As older Charlie's friends had arrived, he made sure that they walked into the lounge, explaining to his friends that their younger selves had been transported from two-thousand and twenty-five, and they were sitting in the kitchen.

They all burst out laughing and would not believe him, saying that they need to call an ambulance because he had lost the plot.

Older Charlie spoke. "You will believe me in a minute, and you will be laughing on the other side of your faces, stay sat down before you fall down!"

Charlie walked off into the kitchen and asked the younger people to go into the lounge. The younger bowlers walked into the lounge.

Their older selves could not believe what was happening, with their former selves in front of them, the older people thought that this was impossible, and thought that they were seeing things, or dreaming about how they could possibly be with their younger version of themselves touching them on the shoulder to see if they were real.

When their older selves noticed Rex and Bruno, they were elated, because the dogs had died years ago, with them making a big fuss of the dogs stroking, kissing, and cuddling them while chatting together, and they talked about their lives and realised that this was really their true younger selves.

Some of them pinched themselves, still thinking that they were dreaming.

The older people explained to the younger people how they had upgraded their eye finger cameras to take and keep still photos, also it had changed from a stun button to a kill button.

The younger bowlers looked and discussed in amazement how good the older people's whistles were dramatically improved.

Their older selves explained in detail that if they stun a person three times they will die, explaining that this protects them against the Mad Magician and his Swifter slaves.

Robert interrupted. "It sounds really excellent, if you get into a life-or-death situation where you need to kill a person, it could save your life!"

Older Darren carried on explaining that the Mad Magician and Umbazan had been transported through a black hole in time from another planet called Drome, which is eleven point eight trillion miles from Earth, which is two light years away.

Younger Charlie spoke. "That is a long way!"

Older Jay explained that they had brought the whistles with them to change the people on Earth into Swifter's, Swifter's have always obeyed the Mad Magician, and Umbazan without question, and they are taught martial arts, and how to kill people on the planet earth, the Mad Magician and his Swifter's are turning people into Swifter's, by touching them on the shoulder with his, and the Swifter's whistles so that they will follow, and fight with the rest of the people to turn more people into Swifter's, so that they can take over planet earth!"

Younger Darren looked shocked. "I don't like the sound of that!"

Older Robert replied. "The Landfawcett lagoon water can turn the Swifter's, The Mad Magician and Umbazan back to normal people if they drink it, or have it thrown on them, so people have been telling us!"

Older Jay changed the subject, noticing that Rex and Bruno must know that it was him because they looked happy to see him.

After they had eaten, Ben commented that he wanted to carry on and find the magnets.

Younger Charlie suggested that they could all help each other along the way.

Robert had a brain wave explaining to use the first letter of their name, and their surname for the older people to make it easier to communicate.

Older Darren laughed. "That will be strange being called Drain instead of Darren, but never mind, I am a calm, and chilled person, I will answer to anything!"

They agreed and discussed how strange the surnames were related to their whistle noises.

JLaugh suggested. "It will be a good idea to use our orange buttons on our whistles so that we can roller skate back to below where Emily was on the sky platform!"

Everybody agreed.

George suggested. "We can ask Emily a few more questions, I am just thinking, why did the brain refuse to take a bath?"

Jake asked. "What is the answer?"

George answered. "Because he didn't want to be brainwashed."

They smiled.

Emily sees them all waving as they skate towards her, waving back, realising that she recognises the older people who live locally.

Everybody blew their whistles, and pressed their black buttons including Rex and Bruno's, with a mash of different strange noises, they then automatically flew up to the sky platform where Emily was standing.

Emily smiled. "Welcome back to the sky platform, it is strange seeing you looking like the double of you, but some of you are older!"

Paul felt a little uncomfortable and shy as usual with her being a girl but still thanked Emily.

Jake asked Emily. "Why does this sign say enter at your own risk in the red quarter of the floor?"

Emily explained. "In the red quarter corner area of the sky platform, people disappear into a secret club, the Mad Magician does not realise that only people with tattoos can enter this area, when the people with tattoos reappear back onto the sky platform, I have not got a clue where they have come from, and I do not ask them anything because this keeps them safe from the Mad Magician!"

Tom suggested to his bowler friends to go into the red quarter to see what was inside of there.

Emily carried on explaining that the older people have special tattoos, they suggested to their younger selves that if they touch them, they will be able to be transported also into the secret club.

All of the younger people touched the older people's tattoos, they then fell down a slide with warm air pushing them down, and they landed onto a soft blue fluffy bean bag.

Darren spoke. "I went to a water park and tried a few water slides, and now I am worried because it is a slippery slope!"

The bowlers laughed.

8

No Tattoo.

The floor had different blues in a swirly pattern, and the room was blowing warm air around, they all walked ahead with Rex and Bruno in between them, there were fifteen screened-off areas with two beds in each section, with clothes hanging over the screens, behind each screen there was a female person massaging men and women in their underwear on comfy soft white fur with gentle music playing, a big whiteboard was on the wall advertising the massaging sessions for free.

Darren pointed out a line of chairs with everybody sitting down to wait for the massaging, talking about how good it was with it being free of charge.

Charlie went first, stripping to his underwear behind the screen, he asked Veronica the therapist about the Magictastic tattoo.

Veronica looked for his tattoo, asking why he had no tattoo, and how could he be there.

Charlie replied. "You may not believe this but me and my friends are from the year two thousand and twenty-five, the only way we were transported into here was through our older selves that already live here that are sitting outside waiting for massages!"

Veronica was in awe, she talked with CPop, and he explained that this was true, and they wanted to help Magictastic to succeed.

Veronica accepted this explanation.

Charlie replied. "I am glad that you believe me!

Veronica told Charlie about the code to the club, explaining that if a Swifter, the Mad Magician, or Umbazan try to enter they will not be able to with their tattoo, because they were detected as evil, as it is a place to enjoy away from evil.

Charlie and his friends thanked Veronica and the other therapists for the massages, and they then carried on walking.

A voice came through the whistles from the Mad Magician, he said that he would cause trouble, and chaos if he found them.

Robert asked the Mad Magician through his whistle why he keeps causing trouble to people's lives and where they live.

The Mad Magician replied in a snappy, aggressive tone of voice. "Because it is what I do!"

PKey commented. "The Mad Magician is horrible!"

The Mad Magician replied. "Our goal is to destroy you all!"

RStorm ended the conversation and said to the group that they would definitely help to destroy the Mad Magician, and they will all work together to eliminate the evil that exists in Magictastic.

In front of Paul, there was a door saying pool party, everybody entered the swimming pool room, swimwear and towels were neatly stacked on shelves, and there was a bar area further on.

Paul commented. "Rex and Bruno look happy to see the water with them walking towards it!"

Robert went to the bar and asked how much the drinks, swimwear, and towels were, with him holding the coin that they had found earlier ready to pay.

The lady behind the bar replied, smiling. "Everything is free!"

CPop commented that a lady was walking towards them, bringing Rex and Bruno some water and dog food, it looked like they had got chips, and a can of Qui being brought to them, and everybody sat chatting and eating.

Jay noticed that there was an artificial large sun hovering in the air above them, and there was also a Jacuzzi and a sauna in the far corner of the room.

CPop spoke. "When I go in a sauna, I normally like to be alone because I have got serious steam issues, but it will be okay today!"

Robert replied. "You are daft!"

Paul noticed and pointed out that steam was rising from the pool, it looked really warm and inviting, and clear water cascaded down into the pool from a blue ridge above, and they were all drinking Blue Rock Cool, they all then decided to get changed and dive into the pool, the walls around the sides of the room had 3D photos with warnings about Umbazan and the Mad Magician.

9

They turned their talk buttons off.

They dived into the pool and swam for an hour, they then went into the sauna for ten minutes, they then got showered, and dressed, and everybody ate cheese pizza with Qui.

Jay spoke. "What is a pizza maker's favourite joke?"

GSing replied. "I don't know?"

Jay giggled. "Slice, slice baby."

Tom chuckled. "Very good."

The Mad Magicians' voice snapped through the whistles. "I am listening, I can get you all when you slip up and go near to the ground, Umbazan will catch everybody and turn you all into my evil Swifter's!"

Jay threatened. "We will stun you all to death!"

Everybody turned off their talk buttons so that the Mad Magician could not hear them, they all walked through the exit door where warm air had lifted them up to the sky platform, the first person that they saw was Emily who said they had been gone two days.

Emily asked. "Did you all enjoy your time in the red club area?"

GSing replied. "Yes, we had fun!"

Jay noticed and pointed out a large group of people looking distant in the eyes, they guessed that they were Swifter's floating up towards the platform, and when they arrived, they realised that they were definitely Swifter's, they were walking towards them.

Jay shouted. "Get ready to attack!"

The Swifter's started to fight the space bowling team, and the bowlers tried to push them off the platform.

Emily was the only person that the Swifter's did not attack back, with the Landfawcett smart flower protecting her from evil.

Tom spoke. "What did the bee say to the flower?"

Chris replied. "What is the answer?"

Tom replied. "Hello, honey."

Charlie replied. "I like that."

GSing and DRain started to laser the Swifter's with their eye fingers.

The Swifter's unsuccessfully attempted to turn them into Swifter's attacking them as well, attempting to touch the Swifter's on the shoulder with their whistles, and people started to get hurt.

Robert started trying to explain to the Swifter's that they were under a spell, but the Swifter's did not listen and carried on saying that they were there to take over the earth with the Mad Magician.

Tom spoke. "Leave now while some of you are still alive!"

The Swifter's were losing the battle with some dead and decided to disappear back down to the ground so that they could regroup.

Everybody was relieved that the Swifter's had left, they looked at how bruised and battered they were.

Emily suggested going to Magictastic to try to stop the Mad Magician's evil before more Swifter's turned up, explaining that the people of Magictastic activate their whistles to fly up and look over the city wall to make sure Umbazan, the Mad Magician, and the Swifter's were not on the other side.

Chris and Charlie asked Emily what the magic hats do and who made them.

Emily explained that the hat looks like a shower cap, and when it is pulled onto the head, the person then thinks of an object, animal or person, and then the person will turn into what they have thought of, when they want to go back to their normal self they just think of themselves and the hat magically turns them into their normal self, if the hat is turned inside out and then placed onto the head, then the hat disappears, and they can think of any size large, or small that they want to be, and the hat will turn them into the size that they have thought of, the hat then disappears back into their whistle when removed from their head.

Jake chuckled. "That sounds amazing, singing in the shower is great until you get soap in your mouth, then it is more like a soap opera!"

Emily laughed. "Very funny, and Darren made the hats and the Smart flower many years ago!"

10

They listened to the singing.

Pkey spoke. "You are clever, Darren."

Emily mentioned that her friend Chloe at Magictastic will also show them around and answer any questions that they may have.

Tom and Robert asked why it was called Magictastic City.

Emily explained that the people of Magictastic City had built it by themselves to fight the Mad Magician, there was a vote to pick the name by the people that live there and the name, City of Magictastic had won.

As they arrived at Magictastic, their whistles were singing, 'Welcome to Magictastic.'

They walked into the garden, and candles were lit everywhere, and food was laid out on the tables.

CLeaf spoke. "Do you know how angels light a candle?"

Pkey replied. "I don't know?"

CLeaf replied. "With a match made in heaven!"

Robert sounded happy. "I love that!"

Rex and Bruno looked happy jumping up and down looking at the food.

CLeaf and Jake noticed that there were small round houses in the perimeter of the stone walls which formed a circle around the garden, families came out to greet them.

Chloe welcomed everybody.

DRain asked why there were so many candles all over the city.

Emily replied. "The candles light the city because the Mad Magician made Umbazan fly the cities four large magnets away, and he has concealed them into a vault that is what we think with the rumours going around, this has taken the power of Magictastic and left them with no electric to give us light, we need you to please save Magictastic!"

Paul asked Emily how the magnets cut off the electricity.

Emily explained. "We put a black plastic slider in between the two magnets to cut the electricity off, as soon as you take the slider out the electricity then returns back to normal, the city had electricity until the magnets were taken away, with two magnets one side of the city, and two magnets at the other side!"

Chris spoke. "I am just thinking we may become more attractive if we ate magnets to pull the ladies in!"

Robert replied. "You wish!"

Chloe interrupted. "Only the 3D map shows you how to get to the city where the wizard Moto lives, he knows the exact spot where the magnets are hidden!"

PKey commented. "I wish the magnet invention to generate electricity had been invented back in two-thousand and twenty-five, our parents would have got free electricity, it would have been brilliant!"

Charlie replied. "I wonder if we could take this idea back to our year and make lots of money!"

Chloe replied. "We are lucky to have Emily with us because she is the only person with a 3D map, this map shows in great detail the position of the magnets!"

Emily and Chloe explained that their 3D map enables everybody to find the Bay Boot calming lagoon, also to find out where Wizard Moto lives, Wizard Moto has got a 3D map with the power signals coming from the magnets in the form of small, short lines protruding up out of the 3D map.

JTrain spoke. "Why are wizards and witches good at English?"

George replied. "Why are they good at English?"

JTrain answered. "Because they are good at spelling."

Chris replied. "You are funny."

Everybody ate some food discussing how dangerous it could be and danced with the Magictastic people drinking too much blue rock cool, and they felt tipsy.

CPop took a photo of everybody on his eye finger.

The bowlers felt tired with them yawning, so they went to bed.

After a good sleep, they talked among each other while eating breakfast, noticing a couple of women opposite stroking Rex and Bruno.

The Mad Magician appeared out of nowhere with his black stone on his whistle glowing making it look super shiny saying I don't like people, they are too much trouble, the Mad Magician touched people on the shoulder with his whistle turning them into Swifter's giving them an evil look on their faces, the Mad Magician attempted to touch Emily, but the smart flower force field protected her from danger.

JTrain shouted. "We need action now, everybody point and press your yellow button on your whistle at the Mad

Magician, all we can do is hope that something will happen for the good!"

This had an immediate impact, and the Mad Magician became frozen, his whistle-stopped glowing and went back to a black stone, everybody dragged him into a room and locked it fighting the Swifter's, and Umbazan at the same time.

Chloe shared her opinion. "I think that the calming lagoon water will make the Mad Magician, the Swifter's, and Umbazan good hopefully!"

The Swifter's carried on attacking everybody, pulling hair, punching, and trying to touch people with their whistles to turn them into Swifter's.

JLaugh stunned the Swifter's, DRain and TBreeze joined in, the Swifter's slowly dropped to the floor lifeless a few at a time.

Everybody set off to the Bay Boot calming lagoon.

Emily and Chloe were leading the way, looking at the 3D map showing the country in detail, hoping that the journey would not be too dangerous, everybody decided to fly, pressing their black button and blew their whistle floating into the air.

Chloe gave instructions. "To move forward, you need to lean forward, put your left arm out to turn left, or your right arm out to turn right, to stop stand up straight and stamp your feet in the air, when stood up straight still in the same position you will float back down to the ground!"

As they flew along, there were different animals to avoid flying over Charlie's house.

The Mad Magician's voice came through the whistles, saying. "I have heard your plans, and they will not work!"

JLaugh yelled. "It did not last long freezing you, at least you're locked up!"

Eric replied. "I have got a joke, what freezes when it gets too hot?"

Harry replied. "What is the answer?"

Eric replied. "A computer!"

Charlie replied. "That was a cool joke!"

George laughed. "I am sorry to interrupt, but he will not be saying that when we get some calming lagoon water in or on him!"

11

I will send Umbazan to kill you.

The Mad Magician shouted down the whistles. "If you give up now, I will not be as harsh to you all, let me out of this room now!"

PKey commented. "You would not be locked up if you were not causing trouble!"

The Mad Magician replied. "You will not trick me to drink any or have any calming water near me!"

ETweet replied. "You, the Swifter's and Umbazan will have no choice!"

The Mad Magician replied. "I am sending Umbazan to kill you all after he has released me!"

Robert commented. "You have picked the right space bowling team; we are determined to sort you all out!"

The Mad Magician replied. "I am out of the locked room now, thanks to Umbazan!"

RStorm and Tom replied. "Why couldn't you have stayed frozen, and we are determined to cure you from evil?"

Nobody heard anything else from the Mad Magician.

Harry spoke. "Do you know why the teddy bear turned down her dessert?"

Robert replied. "What is the answer?"

Harry answered. "Because she was stuffed."

The bowlers laughed and then carried on to the Bay Boot calming lagoon flying back onto the sky platform thinking that it would be easier to get onto the sky rail, they all noticed a sign saying enter into the red quarter at your own risk, with them mentioning that it sounded like the last club.

Harry mentioned that Umbazan would probably not catch them in there, hopefully.

They decided to go in until the sky rail arrived, the younger people touched the older people's tattoos with them all getting transported inside, they noticed that it said rainbow shopping centre above them while walking down the silver glittery staircase into a shop, with it saying dream machine above, with a large piece of glass in a see-through room full of people, some awake, and some asleep with tattoos on their skin.

A girl woke up looking at a small red car coming out through the glass, she then sat in it, it was like a magical illusion.

Rex and Bruno chased the car around then jumped onto the bonnet, trying to stay on for dear life.

After half an hour the car stopped, and there was a notice flashing up on the dashboard saying your dream is over, please vacate collecting your ticket.

The car then disappeared, with Rex and Bruno falling to the floor with a bump.

They all walked over to the girl.

Harry asked the girl. "How did you get the car to come through the glass?"

The girl explained. "My name is Courtney, I fell asleep and dreamed it, I woke up and the dream became reality, there is a raffle, if people win, you can win the opportunity to do what you have dreamed of for life!"

Eric spoke. "Do you know why the little girl took her bicycle to bed?"

Paul replied. "Why would you take a bike to bed?"

Eric replied. "Because he didn't want to sleepwalk."

The bowlers laughed and then fell asleep on the shop floor, including Rex and Bruno.

Charlie and CPop had dreamed that they had won the lotto, when they had woken up a big bath full of Landfawcett money had appeared out of the glass wall, they sat in the money amazed, after a while the bath of money disappeared, and they both fell to the floor, two tickets had appeared in its place.

Eric and ETweet woke up after dreaming about two rare Roga birds, the birds appeared from the wall and landed on each of their arms, they were delighted to see them flying around with a few tickets falling off their pretty precious orange wings, and then the birds had vanished.

Paul and PKey had dreamed of being on television, when they had woken up, a large black television appeared out of the wall, it had no power to it saying step into the television above, they stepped in and became part of the pop concert singing along to the music, all of a sudden they were back in the room with two tickets laid on the floor.

Robert and RStorm looked at a house coming through the glass discussing their future home, maybe if they did win looking around how nice it was, two tickets had appeared on the floor out of the wall, and they picked them up as the house disappeared.

Chris and CLeaf looked at a beach with the sun above the loungers and a waiter coming out, those that were awake sat on the loungers and they ordered Qui and started reminiscing about good times at the Landfawcett bowling centre, after a few drinks everything disappeared, then two tickets appeared out of the wall.

Both Jay's looked at six go-carts on a track that had appeared out of the wall, both Paul's, both Robert's, and both Jay's chose helmets and stepped into the go-carts.

Jay and JLaugh set off first to try to win the race with everybody following, after a while, everybody appeared back inside of the room with a ticket at the side of both Jay's.

Darren and DRain woke noticing a Jenny's Swing book and Jenny's Waltz Learn to Dance book that had come through the wall, all of a sudden everybody woke finding themselves in a silver sparkly dance studio with music playing, just as they had learned the dance everybody had appeared back in the glass room shortly after.

Darren and DRain picked up their ticket.

Ben and BSteps noticed a large blue room full of foam with music coming through the glass, they all danced to the music, and the foam came out to the beat of the music as they all got covered in foam.

CLeaf pressed his orange button on his whistle with everybody copying turning it into a roller disco, after a few songs everybody appeared back in the room of glass with it all gone, and two tickets were left on the floor for them to put into their pocket.

Tom and TBreeze looked up in amazement at a massive high wall coming out of the glass with steps at the side of the wall and safety harnesses for everybody at the top of the platform, everybody awake discussed what Rex and Bruno were dreaming about while climbing the wall, and abseiling down the wall with their harness on discussing how great it was pressing their black buttons and blew their whistles to float up to the top of the platform instead of walking up the steps to save time, as their feet touched the floor everybody appeared back in the glass room where it had all vanished, two tickets were waiting on the floor.

Both George's looked at the wall; a sign said animal hospital above, a nurse, and different animals came out of the wall, people awake started to stroke some rabbits, they bandaged a cats bleeding paws that looked like Suki Chris's cat, just as they had finished a nurse announced that nurse means amme in Danish, with both George's feeling happy to learn a new word in another language like they had always wanted to, everybody ended up back in the room with two tickets on the floor that they had picked up.

Both Jake's got in a helicopter which had appeared from the wall, they excitedly boarded the helicopter and flew around for a while, then came down with a bump back into the room with two tickets ready to pick up at the side of them.

12

They guessed what was coming out of the wall next.

Both Harry's looked up at the wall as a large colourful chocolate and milkshake machine came out of the glass, the people awake walked over to try all of the new chocolate before it went onto the shop shelves, they drank and ate so much they started to feel a little bit sick.

Harry commented saying that he was sure that there was something in the chocolate to make them happy, they all put a chocolate bar in their pocket for later just in time before they ended up back inside of the room with two tickets in it's place, they were disappointed because the chocolate had disappeared from their pockets.

Rex and Bruno looked up at the glass like they knew what was coming out of it, a small colourful obstacle course appeared out of the wall, and everybody awake joined in with Rex and Bruno jumping over the bars around the obstacle course, the dogs were full of energy, and everybody enjoyed themselves.

The bowlers pressed their orange buttons on their whistles to turn their shoes into skates to make it more fun, and then everything disappeared in a split second, leaving two tickets behind for them to pick up.

George saved Rex and Bruno's tickets, folding the corners so that he knew that they belonged to Rex and Bruno.

Emily sat looking up at the glass wall and horses had appeared, there was a large racetrack with a few haystacks for the horses to jump over, they had a horse race around the racecourse hoping that they did not fall off jumping over the hay.

Jake felt very happy that he had won the race; he boasted that his heart was going ten to the dozen with them coming to the finish line, they all fell to the floor finding themselves back in the room with a ticket at the side of Emily that she had picked up and saved inside of her pocket.

Chloe looked up at the glass wall, as an indoor skydiving machine blew them up to the ceiling she said that she had always dreamed of floating up into the air, and going back down when she clicks her fingers, they all followed joining in with excitement, the ceiling was full of sweets with a rainbow of colours, and a chocolate fountain facing down flowing, with chocolate cups for them to drink from on a chocolate shelf, they all agreed that the sweets were fruity and delicious after everybody had a drink they all went with a bang to the floor arriving back in the glass room with a ticket at the side of Chloe.

They all commented that they felt a little sickly while walking into the next room.

Courtney was already in the room, waving at them.

They walked over to Courtney with her explaining while walking about with the tickets that they had in their hands from the glass room that only twelve people would win a dream pocket watch, when the dream pocket watch opens your dream stays alive, and real when the pocket watch is closed, everything disappears back into the watch like it had never existed.

They were getting excited and loud, discussing how exciting it was to see if any of them would win their dream pocket watch.

The man was pulling names out of the virtual hat; he knew everybody's name on all of the tickets.

Chloe congratulated Courtney on winning her dream pocket watch, with the dream locked inside until it is opened.

Only eleven lucky winners were left still to be drawn.

Two strangers won, and then the man shouted for Charlie and CPop to collect their dream pocket watch each, with the man explaining that any money that had not been spent would go back into the pocket watch when it was closed, they were both thinking what they would do with the money, kissing their pocket watches looking very smiley.

Jay and JLaugh collected their dream pocket watch next, looking so happy being able to ride on go-carts again.

There were two pocket watches for Paul and PKey, they looked incredibly happy knowing that they could walk into the television to watch a concert.

The man wished them all good luck; there were only three tickets left to be won.

Jake and JTrain collected their dream pocket watches, meaning that they could have a helicopter ride when they wanted, they whispered to each other how amazing it was with them all agreeing.

Emily was the last to win with her feeling excited about getting onto a horse again collecting her dream pocket watch, they walked back up the glittery steps.

Charlie dragged Rex and Bruno behind them getting back outside into danger back on their journey to find wizard Moto, the four magnets, and the calming lagoon, they crept outside slowly ready to go onto the sky rail, they heard a noise on the ground and looked down.

They noticed that a large shadow covered the sun, the dark shadow below was from Umbazan, he had appeared with his three tails banging below, making holes in the ground.

Umbazan was jumping up to attempt to crush them to death just missing them, they were pleased that the sky rail had arrived.

13

Invisible bubble force field.

They stepped onto the sky rail from the sky platform and sat down and talked about how glad that they were not on the ground, they could now look for the Landfawcett smart flower, the calming lagoon, and the magnets.

Rex and Bruno looked happy, wagging their tails.

Some people got off the sky rail, and a crowd of people got on, it was obvious that they were Swifter's with their evil, dazed and confused looks touching people on the shoulder, with their whistles turning them into Swifter's, while attacking the group the older people in the bowling team lasered the Swifter's and killed them, with more Swifter's appearing towards them, there were too many Swifter's to fight.

Emily had a force field which was an invisible bubble around her, people who tried to attack her bounced off the force field onto the floor, not realising that the smart flower had this power, she was able to touch the Swifter's with her smart flower, and turn them back into normal people one at a time.

Emily saw Jay and Charlie being turned into a Swifter so she immediately ran forward, and touched Charlie with her smart flower, and turned him back to normal, she could not reach Jay, but JLaugh saw what had happened and opened his pocket watch releasing a go-cart.

Jlaugh picked Jay up and strapped Jay into the restraint of the go-kart so that he could not fight anybody.

Everybody else rested on the comfy orange seats with footstools, with them feeling exhausted looking at their wounds.

They went for a walk, finding that there were bacon sandwiches and bottled water at the bar, so they all helped themselves, they then walked back to their comfy orange chairs watching Jay trying to escape from the go-cart feeling sorry for him.

Emily had recovered from her ordeal earlier, she then touched Jay with her smart flower to turn him back to normal, they released him from the go-kart, and he looked dazed for a few minutes.

The bowlers explained what had happened to him, noticing that he was coming back to his old self, chatting away, they said that they were happy to have him back to normal.

Jay got his own water bottle and bacon sandwich.

JLaugh shut his pocket watch, and the go-kart disappeared back inside.

They discussed where they were going next and looked at the 3D map, the instructions showed how to get to Moto when they had left the sky rail, they realised that it was two more stops ahead when they needed to get off, they each got a bottle of water to take with them, the sky rail carried on past the next stop as nobody wanted to get on or off.

Rex and Bruno slept through all of the danger, waking up just in time to depart.

They jumped off the sky platform, also blowing their whistles, and pressed their orange button to float with their skates onto the ground.

Umbazan was waiting to attack them just as they were nearly within reach of the ground.

JTrain opened his pocket watch with his helicopter appearing instantly.

Everybody changed back into shoes with their orange button while jumping onto the helicopter as fast as they could as JTrain flew into the air.

Chloe sounded distressed as Umbazan had bitten her leg as she had jumped into the helicopter, she was looking at her leg with blood running down it, realising that there was a tooth stuck in it which had created a large hole with it making her feel a little queasy.

RStorm reached for the first aid kit, and pulled the tooth out with his fingers, then bandaged her leg.

They flew in the helicopter to Moto to look for the Landfawcett smart flowers and the magnets.

Tom spoke. "Do you know why the toddler threw the butter out of the window?"

George replied. "I don't know."

Tom replied. "So that he could see a butterfly."

They laughed.

The 3D map guided them to a forest full of trees where the calming lagoon was near, the helicopter landed, and they stepped out of the helicopter onto the forest floor.

JTrain shut his pocket watch, making the helicopter vanish back into the watch.

The bowlers were starting to panic as they could hear Umbazan running towards them.

Tom and CLeaf shouted that they could feel his breath on their faces and necks from a distance, they pressed their orange button on their whistles so that their shoes turned into roller skates to get to the calming lagoon faster.

Rex and Bruno ran with them.

Umbazan had flattened GSing with one of his tails.

Rex and Bruno started barking angrily, obviously to try to scare Umbazan with no success.

GSing with his fast thinking put his hat on inside out making him so tiny that he could possibly get away without being seen by Umbazan, they were skating away, shouting to each other deciding what to do next.

Emily changed back to shoes, trying to climb a tree, but fell through the bark into the centre of the tree, everyone followed her out of view of Umbazan.

Inside the tree were several tiny creatures, they looked similar to a caterpillar, but they were bright red talking to the bowlers explaining to them that they needed to go back outside of the tree when Umbazan had gone, as it was only a temporary hideaway.

GSing cried with pain because Umbazan had squashed him with his tail.

They sat on the floor and rested for a while.

Emily looked at the 3D map and realised that the calming lagoon was just around the corner announcing her news.

The bowlers put their hats on the correct way to blend in with the surrounding forest around them before leaving the hideaway, they turned into flowers and trees, moving along slowly towards the calming lagoon.

Umbazan arrived with them and sniffed them all, he looked confused because he could smell them but could not see them, as they slowly walked to the calming lagoon, Umbazan had followed them, they put their hat on inside out, and turned into small people, confusing Umbazan even more, with trees, and flowers vanishing in front of his eyes.

Darren found it funny with him trying not to giggle, attracting Umbazan.

They all giggled, confusing Umbazan even more with laughter coming from different areas.

Umbazan tried to stamp on them, just missing them.

The bowlers grew large again, taking their hats off, with them going back into their whistle pouches automatically, running into the calming water as fast as they could, throwing the water at Umbazan with their water bottles.

Just as Umbazan was about to hurt them, and turn them into Swifter's, he was stood looking confused, they carried on throwing water at him, hoping that it would turn him into a favourable character so that he would help instead of hinder.

Umbazan looked like he did not know where he was.

The bowlers explained to Umbazan that he was not under the Mad Magician's spell anymore.

Umbazan looked like he understood what they were saying to him, with Umbazan nodding his head and sticking his tongue out.

The bowlers walked around Umbazan cautiously with GSing complaining about his pain still.

Umbazan licked them all like he was their best friend.

The bowlers filled their bottles full of calming water, then walked further down where the 3D map showed that the Landfawcett smart flower was next to a tree.

They found the smart flowers, noticing that there were only two smart flowers to protect them from danger available to pick, and they tried to pull the flowers out of the ground with no success.

Umbazan could see what they were trying to do and just pulled the flowers out immediately using his teeth and lips with it having deep roots.

The bowlers realised that they could trust Umbazan now.

Charlie and JTrain put the Landfawcett smart flower into their pockets, agreeing to share the Landfawcett smart flower with each other as needed.

Emily suggested. "I think that we should go back to the sky platform to catch the sky train, it says on the 3D map to get to Bay Boot!"

DRain said to be careful in case the Swifter's were hiding anywhere to attack them, they took the risk of looking around getting onto the sky rail trying to relax on the chairs, with Umbazan running below shaking the ground with loud banging noises as he ran, they took turns to arm wrestle each other for fun.

They looked at the 3D map, noticing that it was another sixteen stops before they got off.

A girl walked down the aisle towards them, asking them what

everybody was doing; she wanted to join in and asked them what the loud banging noise was on the ground below.

The bowlers explained that they were arm wrestling each other, and their friend Umbazan was running below on the ground, making the ground shake as he runs.

14

Emily opened her pocket watch.

Tom asked. "Where are your parents?"

The little girl said that she was going for a walk before her parents started dropping asleep, with her saying that her mum was called Lucy.

JTrain said. "As long as they know where you are, that is OK, what is your name, and how do you know if the ocean is friendly?"

She replied. "How do you know, and my name is Izzie!"

JTrain replied. "It waves!"

Izzie replied. "That is cool!"

They noticed that it was nine stops before they got to Bay Boot.

Izzie had an arm resell with Drain with Izzie winning, thinking that it was awesome.

Drain complimented Izzie. "Well done!"

Izzie noticed that her mother, Lucy, was walking towards them shouting her name.

Charlie noticed that Izzie's mum, Lucy's eyes, looked distant, and evil, thinking that she could be turning into a Swifter.

Izzie walked towards her mother Lucy and thanked DRain for the arm resell.

Izzie's mum started swinging her whistle backwards and forwards, erratically banging into the seats on the sky train, then she was about to touch Izzie on the shoulder with her whistle to turn her into a Swifter as well.

CLeaf realised that Izzie was in danger, throwing calming water out of his water bottle over Izzie's mum Lucy.

Lucy stood still in a trance, changing back to normal.

Izzie looked shocked and a little upset, cuddling her mum Lucy at what had just happened.

A gang of Swifter's were walking towards them.

The bowlers walked down the train in the opposite direction, dragging Izzie and her mum Lucy with them.

Rex and Bruno followed.

Emily, Charlie, and HEm held them back with their force field to keep the Swifter's away from everybody.

They got off the sky rail at the next stop as fast as they could onto the sky platform with a crowd of Swifter's following behind them.

Emily opened her pocket watch with the horses running out stampeding towards the Swifter's, knocking them over.

Emily shut the pocket watch, and the horses disappeared back inside of her pocket watch.

Charlie speaks. "Did you know the other day I heard that a horse walked into a bar, the barman replied with, hey, and the horse replied with, yes please!"

Jay laughed. "You are daft."

The bowlers waved goodbye to Izzie, and Lucy, watching them join Izzie's dad.

Emily looked at the 3D map to find out the way to Moto to look for the wizard Moto.

All of the people that were waiting to get onto the sky rail looked gob-smacked at what had just happened.

They floated down to the ground hoping that the Swifter's did not follow them.

Umbazan was waiting for them calmly at the bottom.

A lady on the ground started to disappear from head to toe, slowly chewing something, they looked puzzled at how she could just vanish.

The lady said. "You will be able to see me properly soon!"

The bowlers saw her arms reappearing.

The lady said. "At least you can see me a little bit now!"

She explained. "It is the chewing gum in my mouth that has made me invisible until I take it out, then I will go back to normal, I have invented and made the chewing gum myself!"

The bowlers asked the lady if she had any spare pieces of chewing gum to make them invisible as well.

The lady replied. "Yes." handing them two tablet-sized pieces of chewing gum to each of them.

The bowlers put their chewing gum into their whistle hat pouches to keep them safe, thanking the lady.

She was just happy to help them.

Emily said, "I am looking at the 3D map, it looks like we do not have that far to travel to get to the magnets!"

Chloe expressed her thoughts that the sooner they got there, the less chance they had of being turned into Swifter's.

Jay noticed and pointed out that the Swifter's were walking towards them, they all started to panic, walking fast to their right.

The Swifter's started to fight the bowlers, the older people fought back with lasers, and the younger people attacked them with their smart flowers, and fists.

The Swifter's that were still alive started to retreat.

After the attack from the Swifter's, they followed Emily.

Umbazan was walking behind them banging his feet, they were nearly at Wizard Moto's house.

They walked past strange-looking stones with a wavy blue pattern on them.

Swifter's reappeared out of nowhere.

Robert shouted, "Put your chewing gum in your mouth everybody now!"

The bowlers chewed their gum and became invisible before the Swifter's could attack them.

Jay placed hats on the dogs to make them small enough to pick them up with his hands.

Rex and Bruno sounded funny with their tiny bark.

CLeaf suggested not hurting the Swifter's and suggested

pouring calming water onto them instead.

15

Darren used his Eye finger.

HEm and Jake laughed at the water dripping from their invisible hands.

Darren spoke. "The other day I heard someone say that a patient had gone invisible, so the doctor said that he couldn't see him at that moment so he would have to wait!"

George chuckled. "You are funny!"

They decided that they needed more calming water.

The water that they had used had immediately turned this group of Swifter's back to normal, with them walking away looking dazed not knowing where to go next.

Tom said. "Ouch, that hurt, who did I just walk into? I have hurt my lip and foot!"

PKey said. "You walked into me, and you have hurt my head!"

They carried on following Emily's voice.

They could hear the Mad Magician's voice through their whistles threatening everybody that they would not go home alive because the Swifter's would kill them.

The bowlers all took their chewing gum out and removed the dogs' hats, and they all turned back to normal.

Umbazan looked at their whistles recognising the voice being familiar, looking puzzled trying to identify his old leader.

They told The Mad Magician to leave them alone, threatening that they would cure him.

Emily informed them that Wizard Moto was just around the corner from them.

Just as they got to Wizard Moto's home, they noticed that there were Swifter's waiting outside.

Paul hid behind a tree, opening his pocket watch.

The Swifter's got distracted by the music coming from Paul's pocket-watch.

Jay sneaked to the door, knocking on it, with Wizard Moto answering.

Wizard Moto walked out with Jay silently, with nobody noticing them.

Darren looked around the trees, with his eye finger to make sure that it was safe; he then shut his pocket watch, as they got far enough away from the Swifter's.

Wizard Moto guided them to the exact position of the magnets.

They asked Umbazan if he could fly the magnets back to Magictastic.

Umbazan nodded up and down, agreeing to help balance the magnets between his three tails.

They flew behind, helping to carry some of the weight of the magnets between them, ensuring that the magnets did not fall waving at Wizard Moto from the air, with him walking back into his home.

Emily shouted instructions from the 3D map guiding Umbazan to the destination of Magictastic.

They flew past the stones to the calming lagoon to refill their water bottles ready to throw the water onto the Mad Magician and the Swifter's.

A group of Swifter's were walking below them.

The bowlers flew down to the ground.

The Swifter's started to attack them with knives grazing a few of them, so the older team lasered the Swifter's to death, in between the smart flower protecting only the people that were holding the flowers from the Swifter's evil powers.

George had blood running down his forehead after being stabbed by a Swifter with the knife catching the top of his head slightly, with blood running onto his eyes making it hard for him to see, he used leaves, and flower petals to mop the blood up from his eyes and face.

They got to the calming lagoon, then refilled their water bottles, they then carried on flying back to Magictastic looking down on the ground noticing that there were two large see-through force fields on the outside of them, there were outlines just visible full of bar code tattoos that everybody had got printed on their skin.

The bowlers discussed that they wondered what they would find while going down onto the ground to investigate further, wondering how to get into the force fields.

The bowlers arrived on the ground and immediately started pouring calming water over the strange force fields with nothing happening.

The only other things that they had thought of doing between them was to laser, kick, and sit on them with no joy as well.

RStorm rested his hand tattoo on the force field.

The force field suddenly burst open, releasing all of the loose tattoos with them floating into the air like a firework curing everybody of evil.

Jay commented. "That sounded like Bruno's whistle being blown with the firework noises!"

Another group of Swifter's suddenly appeared about to attack them with guns, they were about to fire them to kill the bowlers.

A tattoo from the force field hit each Swifter on their hand where their tattoo was, they suddenly looked confused, with their tattoos glowing yellow, and they started asking where their family members were.

The bowlers cautiously walked near to the Swifter's with them explaining what had happened to them.

The Swifter's that they had killed were still lying on the ground dead.

Robert looked at the dead Swifter's, feeling sad that they were dead.

BSteps placed his hand tattoo onto the second force field; a second burst of tattoos flew into the air; the tattoos touched each dead Swifter on their hand; the bowlers watched the dead Swifter's come back to life from lying on the ground in astonishment that they were alive.

The ex-Swifter's looked disorientated, with their tattoos glowing red and yellow.

Darren commented that he hoped that the ex-Swifter's would go back to a normal life.

On their walk back to Magictastic there was a growing gang of people that used to be Swifter's following them.

The bowlers wondered how they would manage to throw the calming water over the Mad Magician.

Robert commented. "It would be good if we could throw it on him when he isn't looking!"

Darren replied. "I wish!"

The bowlers arrived at the sky platform and decided to travel on the sky rail, as Umbazan was managing okay balancing the magnets on his own.

Chloe put Rex's and Bruno's whistles up to their mouths, ready for them to blow.

Everybody floated up to the sky platform waiting for the sky rail causing organised chaos stepping onto the sky rail, and they travelled to Magictastic all crammed in close to one another.

As they arrived at the Magictastic stop, they left the sky train and walked the rest of the way to Magictastic following Emily with her holding the 3D map.

Chris spoke. "What did the fish say when it swam into the wall?"

Darren replied. "I don't know?"

Chris replied. "Dam."

Robert laughed.

As they got there, Umbazan had just arrived before them with the magnets.

Ben spoke. "We have nearly won the battle against the Mad Magician, if we could just get the four magnets back into Magictastic City we have won."

RStorm took a photo on his eye finger of Umbazan being so happy.

The Mad Magician's voice came through the whistles, saying that he would stop Umbazan from bringing the magnets back into the city.

He then went quiet.

The bowlers were worried that the Mad Magician was planning something bad to happen to them.

There was a small forest full of trees outside of the city.

Chris was walking past a tree, and all of a sudden, the tree sucked him in, making him fall over, he was complaining that he was hurt and bruised by the tree's spiky branches.

16

They Looked for the Button.

Chris got up and pushed himself out of the tree, starting to walk away brushing himself off with bits of tree falling from his clothes as he walked.

The bowlers asked if he was okay.

Robert spoke. "I hope that you were not hurt too much!"

They were trying not to laugh at him.

Chris spoke in a troubled tone of voice. "I think that I will be okay!"

They were all walking behind Chris, and they suddenly all got sucked into a black hole in the middle of the same tree that Chris had fallen into earlier, everybody tried to fly away from the black hole in the opposite direction knowing that it was too late because of the powerful force, they were transported to a place that they did not know.

The bowlers noticed a sign saying Planet Drone on it.

CPop spoke. "Do you know how Earth knows that the moon cannot eat anymore?"

George replied. "Give us the answer!"

CPop replied. "When it is full."

Charlie replied. "I like that!"

A man with a D-shaped head appeared, nobody knew him, with them looking at the D on his head strangely; nobody went near him, because they were worried about how safe he was.

The bowlers noticed and whispered to each other that the man with the D on his head was whispering to a man with an A-shaped head, and a man with a Z-shaped head, the letter T head joined in as well.

Robert commented. "This place is strange."

The bowlers wondered what the letter people were talking about with them having a heated discussion about something.

George noticed that CPop was missing telling the others discreetly.

The bowlers discussed that maybe the letter people were secretly talking with the Mad Magician to keep them captive.

The letter C man walked towards them.

The bowlers were worried that the letter people may turn them into Swifter's as well.

The bowlers yelled at Umbazan hoping that he might hear their cry for help and help them out of the black hole.

Suddenly the Mad Magician's voice came through their whistles saying that they will get no help, and they are trapped in prison with the letter people, explaining that the letter people were his secret helpers.

Chris said. "There will be a button somewhere to release us back through the black hole that the Mad Magician uses to get to the Magictastic forest!"

They started to look around the room for the button that should be hidden somewhere in the room.

RStorm and HEm distracted the letters by shouting at them, touching them, and annoying them with everybody else joining in.

Tom walked behind the letter people to look for a button.

The letter D noticed Tom and chased him.

The letter Y grabbed Tom trying to remove his whistle with it not moving; they all began to fight the letter people to keep their whistles.

DRain used his clear amnesia button on his whistle, pointing it at the letter Y.

The Y paused for a moment, everybody thought that it was working, and then the Y carried on because it did not work on him.

CPop appeared out of nowhere, he looked at his eye finger where a photo had appeared of his friends on it, he touched all of his friends on the photo with the palm of his other hand, and this transported him to where everyone was.

CPop helped them by joining in with the fighting.

BSteps got everybody to stun the letter people trying to kill them with no success.

HEm shouted for everybody to run towards him, and touch the photo of Umbazan, hoping that they would appear back with Umbazan.

They touched the photo together, with RStorm disappearing last.

They travelled through time arriving back with Umbazan outside of Magictastic, they walked into Magictastic city together hoping that the Mad Magician was not there.

The Mad Magician appeared out of nowhere, saying that he would damage the magnets that Umbazan was carrying on his back.

Just as he said that everybody got their calming water bottles, throwing them over the Mad Magician with the crowd of people from Magictastic stopping him from moving.

The Mad Magician stood looking confused while the calming water worked, with him starting to ask what was going on, and why he felt helpful and kind again.

They all explained that he had changed for the better because of the calming water, he then helped everybody to put the four magnets back into their home where they belonged on either side of the city with the whole of Magictastic going back to normal, and everybody felt over the moon to have their lives back from a living hell to being calm and normal again.

They partied all night celebrating and drinking too much Blue Rock Cool looking at themselves on the front page of the 3D newspaper being heroes with a big happy drunk looking smile on their faces.

The younger people turned their dials to two-thousand and twenty-five, they were happy that their whistles were there for future dramas, they said their goodbyes to the Magictastic people, giving them a goodbye group hug.

The Magictastic people gave the bowlers a hug, thanking them for their help.

The bowlers pressed their yellow buttons getting transported back to their lives chatting through their whistles on their way back home, still feeling a little bit tipsy, they were glad that they had helped the people of Magictastic to get their lives back to normal.

As they arrived back in twenty-twenty-five, it was like they had never left with it being the same time as they had left sat in the Landfawcett space bowling centre together with the Bay Boot team.

They could tell that something had obviously happened as some people were crying and looked devastated talking about the things that were happening outside, they walked outside to look around.

The World of Present, Future and Past

The Glowing rings

17

They all Picked a Ring out of the Envelope.

The space bowlers were glad to be back in two-thousand and twenty-five, they had walked outside the Landfawcett space bowling centre badly injured, tired and dirty from their last adventure, they were feeling glad that it was nearly the month of May, with them discussing how sunny and warm it was with it making them feel happier.

On their eye fingers, Paul and Jay took a group photo of their friends, and the dogs Rex and Bruno were feeling happy to be back, feeling like the drinks that they had drank in their last adventure had worn off.

Paul was showing off his magical pocket watch from their last adventure.

He was feeling proud because the television appears out of the magical pocket watch, and he was able to step into the television, which had got no power, and became part of a pop concert with them singing along to the music.

George complained about his head being in pain and all of the dry blood from being stabbed.

Chris was concerned about the deep scratches on his body that the spiky tree branches had caused from their last adventure.

An ambulance stopped at the side of them, a lady paramedic introduced herself as Sara and walked up to George and Chris from the ambulance, asking if they needed any help.

They stepped into the ambulance with Sara, where she cleaned and dressed their wounds.

They thanked Sara and joined the rest of their friends.

Robert, Jake, and Chris were disappointed to be home.

Jay started discussing their unexpected, strange adventure that had just happened with his space bowling friends.

Because they all had a whistle, Darren suggested that they had all been watched under cover from a distance for a while before the last adventure had started at the Landfawcett space bowling and ice-skating centre.

Chris spoke. "The other day I heard that a ham sandwich walked into a bar and asked for a drink, but the bartender replied with, I am not serving food today, sorry!"

Paul laughed, setting everyone else off.

Jake commented. "I felt honoured to save the Magictastic people from misery!"

George and Harry looked happy to be home with a big smile on their faces.

The bowlers noticed a medium-sized envelope, noticing that it had got their names written on it in large plain black writing flying into George's face.

Chris caught the envelope in mid-air, just before it hit George, and handed it to Robert.

Robert opened the envelope, inside was a piece of blank white paper and there were rings laid on the bottom of the envelope.

They counted the rings together, noticing that there was a ring each, and three left over.

The rings had star-shaped indented marks on the outside surface.

Each of them picked a ring out of the envelope.

Robert put the envelope containing the paper, and the three spare rings into his pocket.

Nothing happened when they put the rings on.

They had tried to take the rings off without success; they were stuck like super glue to their fingers, and their whistles were still stuck around their necks.

Eric and Paul were excited, and they wanted another adventure.

Jake looked scared and blurted out loudly that he thought that something would happen because the rings were stuck to them.

They walked into the newsagent shop with the dogs Rex and Bruno keen at their heels with Charlie speaking. "Do you know why the scarecrow won a reward?"

Jake replied. "I don't know?"

Charlie answered. "Because he was outstanding in his field."

The bowlers laughed with the man behind the counter, staring at them for a second.

Robert noticed a lady reading a newspaper inside of the shop, it was dated the first of May twenty-twenty-five, she was crying and muttering that there would be no more trees to make newspapers or furniture for the future generation.

The grumpy man behind the counter, with no smile on his face, told them to take the dogs outside.

They ignored the man with Rex and Bruno barking at him.

He scanned the lotto ticket that Charlie had bought for his mum before the last adventure had begun.

The man behind the counter looked frightened of Rex and Bruno, he was looking at them cautiously and nervously shaking slightly while he was scanning the ticket.

The man had a shocked look on his face with his jaw dropping, and his eyes nearly popping out of their sockets.

He could hardly speak stuttering his words announcing the good news, hearing a loud jingling bell from the till

that Charlie's mum had won nine
hundred million pounds.

Charlie fell over in shock,
breaking a shelf full of biscuits; he stood
up with help from Darren, feeling elated
for his mum while moaning about his
arm hurting at the same time.

The man offered to send the ticket
off and cash the ticket in for Charlie's
mum for his share of two million
pounds for his troubles.

Charlie laughed, then declined the
offer, moving away from the counter for
a moment, discussing to his bowler
friends that he felt a little mean saying
no, as he could get as much money as he
liked from his pocket watch whenever
he needed it.

Tom said that somebody needed to run the shop and if he had that much money, the shop might close, making Charlie feel a little bit better.

The man gave Charlie the lotto ticket back, and just as they were about to walk out of the shop, the man noticed the rings commenting how different they looked.

They agreed with the man, saying how unique they were and how they had found them in the envelope earlier.

The man explained that Charlie's mum needed to call the number on the ticket to arrange a cheque.

The bowlers walked out of the shop, they were feeling excited to share the news with Charlie's family.

Outside of the shop, they noticed a queue of vehicles driving behind each other and they also could hear loud gunshots and people screaming, and different parked abandoned vehicles that people had already vacated.

The bowlers hid behind a skip out of view from the shooters.

They used their eye fingers pointing them around the corner to watch what was going on out of view, with them feeling shocked at what they were seeing.

A man stood at the side of the bowlers behind the skip with them, he was whispering that the Windowir's were at it again.

The bowlers asked the man what he was talking about.

The man replied that he only knew the name from the rumours going around.

They watched the horror unfold in front of them.

Innocent people were running away from people with glass hats, and strange-looking guns.

The bowlers used their eye-finger cameras to enlarge their view of the bullets and guns, and they noticed strange glass bullets with short needles on the end leaving the guns shooting towards them, the bullets shaved past some people just missing them, with others not so lucky.

Shattering glass was all around them from the shop, and house windows with people running away.

Loud crunching noises from the glass under their feet could be heard as they ran away from danger.

Jay and Ben found small, clean pillows.

Darren and Tom tied the pillows with some soft fabric that they had found to the soles of the dogs' feet and legs so that they could walk on the glass without cutting themselves.

The bowlers dare not move from behind the skip, still watching helplessly.

Some unlucky people didn't manage to get away because their black guns had got sharp needles attached to the bullets sticking into people's skin, the bullets then released glass and formed a glass spiders glass web around the body area that the bullet had hit with the web travelling up to their heads, and it had created a transparent glass hat on their heads.

The bowlers noticed that the hats looked heavy, making their heads tilt a little; they then went into a trance, walking behind the shooter into a brightly lit door that had appeared, then disappeared in a flash behind them.

They cautiously left from behind the skip noticing that people were looking at their own vehicles, shaking their heads in disgust that their vehicles were trapped, and they were not able to move them because some glass had punctured their tyres, and some of the drivers must have been taken away by the shooter, with some vehicles having no driver.

The bowlers started asking people what was going on.

People looked frightened with not many people wanting to talk because they were upset with tears rolling down their faces, and they had obviously known some of the people that had been taken away.

They noticed the man that was with them behind the skip had walked away.

Different people explained while walking away that Tiger, Vord and the Windowir's from planet Opack were evil, taking over peoples bodies and imprisoning them without their consent changing them into Windowir's, needle bullets were destroying the trees, plants, insects and animals causing them to die, people were becoming very ill in certain places with the lack of nature.

The bowlers asked people about Tiger, Vord and the Windowir's.

People only knew their names because they had heard the Windowir's mentioning their names before.

Suddenly a brightly lit doorway appeared again with people shooting people that could not hide away in time, and took more people away, with a brightly lit doorway appearing from nowhere, and the newly formed Windowir's followed the lead shooter through the door, which then vanished behind them.

The bowlers looked shocked that this could happen again.

They travelled forward in time to twenty-fifty-five to get their future selves to help them.

Ben and Jay informed the rest of the team through their whistles that they had made a mistake with their dials landing in twenty-seventy-five.

The rest of the bowlers in twenty-fifty-five moved forward in time to twenty-seventy-five with them previously arranging to meet at future Paul's house with them finally arriving.

They talked about all of the changes that they had noticed along the way to Paul's house.

Chris noticed houses that were made of bricks and were hovering above the ground like a balloon, he pointed out that a house gradually lowered to the ground and a person had walked inside.

They were in disbelief at what they had just seen.

Robert spoke. "Do you know what lights up a football match?"

George replied. "I don't know."

Robert answered. "A football match."

The bowlers laughed.

Jay noticed and pointed out a bin wagon below them with it out of control, with a brightly lit doorway appearing, and the bin men were following the shooter into the doorway commenting that the situation was worse than they had thought.

They all agreed.

The bowlers discussed along the way that in twenty-seventy-five, their future selves could have children.

Robert commented. "We would be more likely to have lovely grandchildren!"

They conferred how nice it would be to unexpectedly meet their future grandchildren if there were any.

George commented that they may have no children.

They arrived at older Paul's home, noticing that it was on the ground.

They looked through the lounge window and noticed Paul's older self with a younger boy about their own age, around fourteen to sixteen years old.

Older Paul and the boy were sitting together looking at Older Paul's pocket watch, chatting about it loudly.

The bowlers heard older Paul calling the young boy Philip through the open window with him still speaking loudly.

In the lounge, Philip asked older Paul if he would open up his pocket watch.

Older Paul opened his pocket watch with a television appearing, they entered the television with the pop concert making many vibrations on the floor from the music.

Older Paul and Philip looked happy together, chatting about old times from older Paul's adventures with his friends and how much he had enjoyed it.

Ben whispered to Jay saying that older Paul's pocket watch still worked and looked as good as it did years ago.

Paul looked hopeful, mentioning that the other person at the side of older Paul could be his future grandchild; he was delighted at the thought of this.

Jay agreed in shock, wondering if this was true.

To not cause confusion to older Paul and Philip.

Jake opened his pocket watch, releasing his helicopter, ready to fly away fast if the situation was awkward.

Older Paul and Philip re-entered his living room and shut his pocket watch with the television, and concert-going back inside noticing the helicopter and the bowlers outside of the window about to stride into the helicopter.

Older Paul knew that it was his past self with just seeing their faces bringing back great memories; he opened the window and shouted for them to come back.

Philip shouted. "Please put the helicopter back in the pocket watch, instead of on the parcark space!"

Getting his words mixed up.

Older Paul explained that Philip meant car park, and he could not say it.

Jake shut his pocket watch, with the helicopter re-entering inside.

The bowlers walked inside of Paul's older selfs house.

Philip said bonne nuit, thinking that it was a posh word.

Paul explained that bonne nuit means goodnight in French, explaining that he had repeatedly told Philip that he should not say that word in the day because people look at him strange that understand what it means.

The bowlers were shocked that Paul still lived there and commented on how well he looked.

Older Paul explained that he lived in the same place in case this amazing situation may happen, with him looking pleased as punch that his dream was happening.

Jay spoke. "I am really pleased to be here!"

Older Paul introduced Philip to Paul, commenting that Philip was his grandchild in twenty-seventy-five.

Both older and younger Paul decided to blow their whistles together, listening to the jingling keys noise laughing and feeling happy with the unique noise together.

The bowlers spoke to Philip and older Paul; they fired plenty of questions towards them about how their lives worked out in the future.

They looked at Jay's eye-finger photo on Paul's pocket watch from earlier in between chatting.

Philip found it very strange that Paul was his younger grandad.

A young boy and girl entered the front door shouting. "Hello!"

Older Paul introduced Ray to Jay, explaining that Ray was his future grandchild.

Jay gave Ray a hug in shock, not knowing what else to do, feeling gob-smacked at this strange and unexpected news.

Older Paul then introduced Cara to Charlie, explaining that Cara was Charlie's grandchild.

Charlie shook hands with Cara, chatting for a while about the news with a disbelieving look.

Older Paul, Cara, Philip, and Ray looked so happy to see Rex and Bruno alive and well again in front of them, with them being able to stroke them, they discussed how good they were.

Darren explained why Rex and Bruno's feet were protected.

Jay pointed out to everybody in shock that older Paul's pocket watch was still ticking.

They listened to the ticking for a second.

Older Paul told the bowlers that older Charlie had invested in streets full of houses and he rents them to people at a low cost.

Charlie felt happy with this news.

They were worried about older Robert not answering the door earlier.

Ray emotionally asked Jay. "Will you please call me Grandad Ray?"

Jay was very delighted to be called grandad.

The bowlers said that they would help to find older Robert.

Tom noticed a newspaper clipping in a photo frame on the table, it had Darren and his live animal playing cards making animals come alive, with cards and the smart flower, with his award certificate in his hand.

Darren looked happy to see the newspaper clipping of himself saying. "I found a newspaper from a 1953 newspaper it said, what do naughty girls become?"

Eric replied. "What was the answer, please!"

Darren replied. "Mummies."

The bowlers laughed.

18

What do the Oil, Water, and Glass Buttons do on the Whistles?

The younger people still looked a little bit confused, not one hundred percent sure if this situation was really happening, or if it was just a dream.

The bowlers had a discussion about all of the problems in twenty-twenty-four.

Philip decided to call Paul, grandad Paul, and Cara started calling Charlie, grandad Charlie.

Cara mentioned that it was like going down memory lane with the conversations between her older grandad, and his friends over the years.

Eric changed the subject, noticing that three extra buttons had appeared on his whistle, one button said glass, another said water and the other said oil.

The rest of the bowlers had got three extra buttons on their whistles, including Rex and Bruno's as well.

Philip could not understand why the three extra buttons were not on older Paul's whistle with him looking a little bit confused.

Cara, Ray, and Philip wished that they had a whistle each, with the glass water and oil buttons as well.

When older Paul had heard that they needed help in twenty-twenty-five with freight in his voice, he immediately offered his help with a big gulp in his throat.

Older Paul suggested that Ray, Philip, and Cara may be better off going to twenty-twenty-five instead of himself with them having faster actions, and them being younger.

Older Paul explained that he felt that he was too old, tired, and vulnerable with him being sixty-six and the unpredictable challenging situations ahead of them.

They talked about older Robert with older Paul ringing him with no answer, with him worried about him wondering if he was okay.

Jake asked older Paul why the houses floated in the air before the friends left on their new adventure.

Older Paul replied. "The homeowner of the houses has got a hover mode option to float up into the air with a sensor warning, it works by a word, light, a blink of the eye or both depending on the settings with them connected to a phone, iPad, laptop, etc.

This warns the homeowner of any people, or objects near to the house that should not be there with an alarm noise, or a voice saying what or who is there.

The owner then decides if they want to lower the house to ground level to let people inside.

They thanked Older Paul for the information and said that they would make sure that Older Robert was found safe and also told Older Paul to try not to worry about Older Robert.

The bowlers begged older Paul one last time for his help, explaining that his stun button would be a great help to stun the Windowir's to death.

Older Paul declined and waved goodbye, saying that he would see them again soon, hopefully in a troubled tone of voice.

They started to walk away slowly.

Older Paul mentioned that they could do with the 3D map from their last adventure for help with navigation to help them along the way.

They shouted back that they would work it out where they needed to go as they lost sight of older Paul.

Ray suggested going back to twenty-twenty-four to stop the Windowir's before all of the shooting had begun.

They agreed.

Robert got the envelope containing the three rings, and the paper out of his pocket, he gave a ring each to Ray, Cara and Philip.

They looked at the rings in detail, discussing how different, and strange they looked in a good way.

They put them on.

Robert put the envelope and the blank paper back into his pocket.

Eric, George and Jay each grabbed Ray, Cara, and Philip's hands.

They changed their whistle dials to twenty-twenty-four, then pressed their yellow buttons, including Rex and Bruno's.

They watched the years flash by in a quarter of a second, arriving in twenty-twenty-four together looking around, and they noticed a sign saying Landfawcett Park in front of them.

Eric spoke. "Let's go into the Landfawcett Park and why is the grass so dangerous?"

Cara replied. "Why is the grass so dangerous?"

Eric replied. "Because it is full of blades!"

Philip laughed, setting everyone else off.

They entered the park noticing trees all around them, with some trees having needle bullets stuck in the bark, with them looking closely at the bullets, and some small sharp needles were connecting to the bark of the tree, with spider webs hanging down from the bullets.

The bowlers had a discussion working out that they thought that whatever the needles touched, including people or items, they were sending out an evil poison or power of some sort.

Leaves fell from the trees covering the bowlers because the trees were dying, they realised that Landfawcett needed help immediately, and they did not know what to do next.

Cara, Philip, and Ray looked shocked at how different everything looked around Landfawcett with the sky train missing, no 3D newspapers, and nobody had got a tattoo.

Philip mentioned that himself Cara, and Ray went into the Landfawcett bowling centre often in twenty-seventy-five.

Darren pointed out that their younger selves would be going into the Landfawcett Space bowling centre for a game later in the day.

19

Space bowlers looked at them
with them having different people with them.

They discussed that they needed to go into the Landfawcett space bowling centre at that exact moment in time for a game, a drink and food, not to cause confusion of people seeing identical people later.

They arrived walking into the space bowling centre through the double doors.

Cara, Philip, and Ray looked shocked at how different it all looked inside and outside.

The other space bowlers already in the building looked at them strangely with them having grazed skin and dirty clothes from their last adventure.

Lezley behind the bar said. "Hello." to them, looking a little confused with them being there at a different time of the day with three different people.

Philip shouted Bonne nuit back to Lezley.

Lezley looked at Philip with a puzzled look.

A lady bowler that knew what Bonne nuit meant asked Philip why he was going to sleep.

Darren changed the subject, ordering food with a slight chuckle.

Cara suggested that they used the showers to get clean now that they had finished eating, with them being smelly and dirty.

Tom spoke. "Did you know that family in Spanish means familia?"

Ray replied. "We do now, we are like a family together!"

They all agreed with Cara, Philip and Ray sat outside the changing room door on a bench, while the bowlers stepped into the Landfawcett changing room showers fully clothed to get clean, they then dried off the best that they could with other peoples towels left on the benches, they were still a little bit wet, discussing how cold they felt and if they should play one space bowling game before they left.

A large door-shaped light appeared out of nowhere outside of the changing room in the doorway near to where Cara, Philip and Ray were sitting on the bench.

Ray warned the bowlers in the changing room by knocking on the door and shouting inside to tell them that the Windowir's were outside of the door.

The bowlers panicked.

Tom looked around the door with his eye finger, noticing that the Windowir's were about to walk inside announcing his news.

The bowlers were attempting to make a small barricade with anything that they could find, including towels, putting them in the doorway attempting to stop the Windowir's entering inside.

Cara, Ray, and Philip hid behind different walls away from the Windowir's.

A leader appeared shooting people, with a group of people following the leader that had been shot in minutes, people that were shot looked distant in the face with web travelling up their bodies from the bullets forming into glass hats.

The line of Windowir's entered the changing room stumbling over the barricade, the bowlers hid next to both sides of the wall next to the door, and they pushed the Windowir's.

The Windowir's fell onto the floor, still shooting at the bowlers just missing them, with the needle bullets hitting the showers behind them having water spraying into the room like a waterfall from the burst pipes making the floor slippy underfoot.

The bowlers distracted the Windowir's by throwing anything that they could find, mainly towels at the

Windowir's with some falling on their heads and smothering their faces and making them pass out onto the floor noticing the water surrounding their bodies, the bowlers ran past the Windowir's grabbing Philip, Ray and Cara on the way outside of the centre using their eye fingers to peep through the window noticing a large flash with a brightly lit doorway appearing.

Philip, Cara, and Ray explained that hiding behind a wall had worked for them.

The bowlers noticed through the window on their eye fingers that the Windowir's from the changing room had woken up, and they were walking down the corridor with water dripping from them, there was also a train of new

Windowir's with glass hats forming on their heads following behind the leader through the lit doorway in a trance inside of the corridor.

They were happy that the Windowir's had left the area but sad that there were more victims taken away, they decided to investigate another city called Jolt, on the way they noticed a few more trees that had fewer leaves than they should have, noticing needle bullets sticking into them, discussing the major problems.

A tall slim teenage girl with blond, short hair stepped out of her front door looking at a tattoo on her finger not looking where she was going; she nearly knocked Eric to the floor, she could not apologise enough to Eric introducing herself as Penny, she blushed like a beetroot walking with the bowlers.

Darren and Tom noticed and pointed out that her tattoo on her finger was identical to their rings.

Cara questioned her how she had got a tattoo the same as their rings.

Penny replied. "I was going for a walk, it had just appeared on my finger a minute ago, I was looking at it, and that is why I had bumped into Eric!"

Darren mentioned how strange it was the tattoo appearing.

Penny explained that she had heard them talking about the trees getting damaged through the open window, and wanted to know more, pointing out again that she did not mean to bump into Eric.

Eric could not stop looking at her, commenting how pretty she looked and did not know what to say, so he smiled blushing with red, rosy cheeks introducing himself.

Then the rest of the bowlers also introduced themselves while looking at Penny and Eric, looking at each other passionately like they wanted to kiss, explaining that they were trying to solve a life-or-death critical situation.

Penny insisted on helping them, following the bowlers travelling on their journey to Jolt city speaking. "I know this is strange because we have just met, but I feel like a snowflake because I feel like I have fallen for you already like we have clicked together Eric!"

Eric replied. "Me too, I think that we must be made for each other like love birds!"

Tom spoke." Sorry to break up your sloppy moment, it is nice to have you with us!"

Penny mainly talked with Eric, mentioning that she was scared of being taken away by the Windowir's.

Eric reassured Penny, giving her a hug, saying that they would get rid of the Windowir's together while looking at her ring tattoo in detail.

Jay commented. "I can see a romance definitely blossoming here!"

Penny loved stroking Rex and Bruno along the way.

Robert spoke to his future grandchild Ray while walking along towards Jolt, discussing how worried that they felt about older Robert.

Darren suggested that they flew instead of walking, the bowlers grabbed hold of Cara, Philip, Penny, and Ray's hands, and they pressed their black buttons including Rex and Bruno's making sure that Rex and Bruno's whistles were near to their mouths as well and then blew their own whistles.

Charlie led the way flying through the air over and around the houses, with people looking at them astonished that they could fly, some people asked them for a lift to see what it was like to fly trying to grab hold of their hands.

It was obvious Eric and Penny liked each other by the way they kept looking at one another passionately while holding hands with Eric speaking. "Let's do a crime together, I will steal your heart, and you can steal mine!"

Penny replied. "I think that we have already stolen each others' hearts!"

Darren replied. "You are so cute together, and what did one volcano say to the other volcano?"

Tom replied. "What is the answer?"

Darren replied. "I lava you."

They laughed.

As they arrived at Jolt city, they noticed nothing different from the last time that they were there apart from an odd random broken window, and bits of glass on the pavements quizzing people if they had seen anybody different, or any strange behaviour out of the ordinary.

A girl introduced herself called Charlotte; she started mentioning that she had seen a group of people that had been shot with needle bullets, with spider webs growing up their bodies forming glass hats on their heads, with them following a lead gunner through a large brightly lit white doorway that had appeared in a split-second flash, the doorway disappeared behind the last person that had entered.

The bowlers realised that there was a pattern of the same thing happening over and over again.

Cara commented. "I feel frightened for my life!"

The bowlers also shared their concerns.

Charlotte explained that she had heard the leader of the Windowir gang mentioning the next town called Jargin, just before he had vanished through the brightly lit doorway.

Tom commented loudly. "That means that Jargin town is next on the Windowir's list!"

The bowlers discussed how they felt frightened for the Jargin town residents and visitors.

Charlotte noticed and commented positively about Rex, and Bruno walking a little bit strange with their pillow feet, and what a good idea it was to protect their feet from any sharp objects.

As the bowlers were about to carry on walking, Darren noticed a bright flash with a door shape in front of them, pointing it out to the rest of the bowlers.

A small gang of Windowir's with guns in front of them came out of nowhere about to shoot them, the bowlers ducked, with the bullets hitting people behind them.

Charlie and Philip tried to tackle the guns from the Windowir's hands, with them nearly grabbing hold of them.

Jay pressed the amnesia button on his whistle, pointing it towards them, making the Windowir's look confused for a moment.

A loud voice came through their whistles, saying. "Shout Zon."

The Windowir's woke pointing their guns at the bowlers, bullets were hurdling towards them as they shouted. "Zon."

20

They looked at the person that they wished to swap their thoughts with.

A man appeared, pushing them onto a soft large, deep, soft padded slide with bright lights above their heads.

The bowlers realised that it was most likely to be Zon with them waving at him, as they entered and dropped, the slide was covered in a clear smooth oil to help them travel faster away from the bullets.

Penny and Eric held hands trying not to slide apart, they finally arrived at the bottom with a door saying. 'Please enter.'

Cara commented happily. "It was good with the oil on the slide, with it making us fall faster!"

They moaned about how oily and disgusting their bodies felt.

Tom suggested putting their vanishing chewing gum in so that they could not be seen if there was danger ahead.

They struggled to put their chewing gum into their mouths with their hands being so wet and oily.

Tom, Eric, Robert, and Jake gave their spare piece of chewing gum to Cara, Philip, Penny, and Ray, with them also struggling to put the chewing gum into their mouths.

As they put it into their mouths, their faces were so funny with the disgusting oily taste, they finally vanished from sight.

Charlie had turned Rex and Bruno's shower hats inside out, placing them onto the dog's heads, making them change from their normal size to a tiny size with them just visible to the eye.

Jay carried Rex in one hand, and Bruno in the other.

They entered the room with oil flowing onto the floor, walking inside trying not to step on each other, with them being invisible.

Chris suggested, pressing the oil button on their whistles to see what would happen.

They pressed their oil buttons with oil ejecting from different parts of their bodies, including their mouths, with the oil flowing onto the floor.

Ray, Penny, Cara, and Philip were covered in oil; they coughed a lot of oil out and slid about underfoot.

Eric held Penny's hand, attempting to help to stop her from falling.

As they slid along, they noticed a bright orange sign above them saying swap tank.

Eric felt tense, not knowing what would happen next, kissing Penny with love.

They cautiously walked into the room noticing a smart and tidy room full of comfy seats, it looked cosy and inviting, and they felt a bit more at ease removing their chewing gum and removed Rex and Bruno's shower caps.

Jay put Rex and Bruno's shower caps away in their whistles, making Rex and Bruno turn back into their correct size again, they then saved their chewing gum in their whistles for later.

A single star in each ring lit up pink, including Penny's tattoo, they could not stop looking at Penny's tattoo ring in amazement, discussing how it had lit up pink as well.

Eric kissed the top of Penny's hand.

Jay mentioned that the ring maybe means something else, with all of the rings lighting up.

There was a man with a name badge saying Bill on his top that were stood in front of them, with him explaining to think of the person next to them, or opposite them, they would then swap memories, or thoughts with that person that they think of.

Bill looked at the lit-up rings, asking why they were lit up pink.

The bowlers explained how they had found the rings in an envelope with no pink lights, the pink lights had just appeared lighting the rings up, explaining that they did not know why.

Bill changed the subject, explaining that the swap would only last for around half an hour at the most.

They exchanged looks, swapping their thoughts in their heads between each other.

Charlie swapped with Rex and Bruno, thinking that all they wanted to do was to sleep and chew on a bone.

They had weird facial expressions looking strange at what each other were thinking.

Harry explained Paul's thoughts that Eric and Penny were from different years, so how could they fall in love, and stay together?

Tom swapped with Penny, realising how much she liked Eric.

Darren, Eric, and Ben were thinking about their safety and how to dispose of the Windowir's.

Jake, Philip, and Cara were thinking of ways to cure the Windowir's somehow.

George and Chris were thinking about the kindhearted ambulance lady Sara who had stopped to help them earlier.

Ray and Penny were thinking about all of the happy things that had happened over the years in their lives.

Harry snapped photos of everybody's different strange faces, including himself on his eye finger to capture the moment of them all exchanging thoughts.

Paul looked at his future grandchild Philip as they were both thinking the same thoughts about each other, hoping nothing drastically bad happens, or Philip, Cara and Ray would not be born in the future.

Robert thought that Chris's ideas were good, but strange.

Robert announced that Chris was thinking of a gun full of grease, so that they could shoot the Windowir's, Tiger and Vord so that they could not hold their guns, with them sliding out of their hands.

Jay loved Robert's idea to be able to shrink anything, with a sprinkle of powder from a tiny bag, and then transport the items from the future, or the past in the palm of his hand to any year that he desires, and then sprinkle the items with the powder to enlarge them again.

After an hour the swap wore off, with the pink lights flickering, the rings had gone back to normal, with no pink lights.

The bowlers walked out of the door waving bye to Bill, thanking him, with Rex and Bruno straggling behind.

As they walked out of the room, they looked up, noticing that there was the sky above them.

Jake opened his pocket watch, releasing his helicopter, with them all stepping on, with Rex and Bruno getting on last with Robert.

They then flew off with them discussing their mixed emotions, feeling amazed at what had just happened, and overwhelmed, with other people's information, and ideas on their minds with them landing, they then exited the helicopter.

As they were back on the ground, they left the helicopter with Jake shutting his pocket watch, the helicopter immediately re-entered inside.

Robert mentioned that it must be Tiger, Vord and the Windowir's who were attempting to slow them down by trying to hurt them.

Charlie suggested that it must be Zon who was fighting against Tiger, like a tug of war to help them.

They travelled to Jargin flying along, with any remaining oil falling off them into each others faces, with some oil landing on people below, with them shouting up how revolting it was, in shock noticing them flying through the air, as they were travelling through the air they had no choice but to fly into a large jar with it closing tight behind them trapping them inside.

The indented stars in the rings lit up blue with them wondering around the jar noticing that it was full of tiny soft flexible squashy jam jars, with the different items inside each jar, some had no items inside floating about in the air, with stick insects and leaves stuck around them.

Robert mentioned that Zon's team must have grabbed the leaves before the trees had started to die for the stick insects to eat.

Each of the bowlers picked up a jar; they looked puzzled at the stick insects attached to the jars.

Darren had picked up a jar saying cheesy feet on it, full of a green fog inside.

Jay commented that Darren's jar was definitely not to be opened with the vulgar pong that would be ejected!

Robert picked up a jar full of strong sweet-smelling strawberry sweets; they were covered with sugar on the outside.

Robert and Harry unsuccessfully attempted to open the sweets.

Eric noticed a sign on the bottom of his jar that he had picked up saying. 'This jar only opens up when it is ready.' With a blue smiley face under the writing.

Paul looked puzzled at what this meant.

Jay looked confused with an empty jar saying. 'Bottled up kids energy on the outside.'

Jake looked confused with a rope inside of his jar.

Cara picked up a jar full of darts.

Philip picked up a jar with a mini brain inside.

The bowlers discussed that only a brainless person would put all of the items into separate jars.

All of the stick insects jumped onto their shirts, automatically sticking to them like glue.

The bowlers tried to knock the jars off unsuccessfully.

Charlie looked confused about his empty jar at what it was saying. 'Hover on the outside of the jar.'

The bowlers noticed that at the other end of the large jar that they were stuck inside, there was another room that had appeared for them to enter into, they agreed that they hoped to look at the rest of the tiny jars later as Chris, Tom, Ben, George and Ray, could not make their mind up which jar that they wanted to pick from the room.

Just before they had left the large jar, Robert snapped a selfie photo of them all on his eye finger just before they had left the tiny jars behind.

The bowlers noticed a sign with Ben reading it. "Enter at your own risk!"

As they entered the room, there was a Jargin newspaper on the table in front of them with a smell of smoke like bonfire night coming from the paper.

Ben spoke. "That reminds me, what do you call a duck that likes watching fireworks?"

Charlie replied. "What is the answer?"

Ben answered. "A fire Quacker."

They all laughed.

Eric picked up the newspaper with everybody standing looking and touching him on the shoulder, trying to look at what he was reading.

George pointed out that he had noticed smoke rising from the top of the page, they read the article together, falling over each other about a bridge burning on the second page, with people trapped, crying, with their clothes getting burnt.

Robert pointed out that flames were starting to dance around the sides of the newspaper.

Eric dropped the newspaper with the heat with them still reading, and then all of a sudden, they started getting pulled into the newspaper column that they were reading, feeling the burning heat from the flames on their bodies, and the smell of burning was very strong.

Ben spoke. "This is scary with us being stuck in the middle of the burning bridge, fearing for our lives among other people screaming!"

Ray spoke. "This is a major emergency now; how can we survive this?"

They were panicking so much, discussing what to do next, saying goodbye to each other, and feeling terribly upset with how hot the flames were with them, causing burn marks on their clothes.

Eric protected Penny from the flames with his body nearly crying with the elevated temperature of the burning heat.

George suddenly had an idea, making Robert get the photo back up on his eye finger that Robert had taken in the large jar room full of the tiny jars earlier.

Robert spoke. "Okay, I will." with fright in his eyes and a tear rolling down his face.

George asked them all to touch the photo.

As soon as they touched the photo, they immediately got transported back into the jar room in the same position, just before they had left the large jar room earlier.

They sighed with relief to be safe again, hugging each other wiping tears away, looking and smelling the burn marks on their clothing, and discussed how lucky they were to be alive and not burnt to death.

Eric whispered sweet nothings into Penny's ear, stroking her hair with them being glad to be safe together with him speaking. "If you were a hot potato, you would definitely be a sweet one."

Penny cuddled Eric.

Chris picked up a jar with gale force winds written on the side.

Tom picked up a jar with a pair of reading glasses inside.

Eric pointed out that they looked like normal reading glasses.

Ben picked up a jar with happy tears written on the side.

George picked up a jar with memories written on the side, looking at it strangely.

Jay looked at George's jar weirdly, with it looking like it had water inside.

Ray picked up a jar with music written on the side, wanting it to break open so that they could listen to music, they tried to release the jars from their clothes again, not wanting stick insects, and useless jars stuck to them unsuccessfully.

As soon as Ray had picked up his tiny jar from the shelf looking at it, they immediately got ejected with a strong warm wind behind them blowing them away like they should not be there, landing in a corridor with a door in front of them, with the best hairdressers award prize evening written on it.

Penny and Cara happily commented that they could do with a hair makeover.

They were stood in front of a door with no choice but to enter the room with no other door available to enter, as they walked through the door, they were stood on a stage with a large audience staring at them, the look of shock on the bowlers' faces was a picture.

A man standing next to them on the stage introduced himself as 'Alf.'

Philip said Bonne nuit to the audience nervously, and the rest of the bowlers said. "Hello." To the audience.

There was lots of laughter in the audience from what Philip had said, and small thin plain white pens were spread out on a table with a cinema screen above with themselves and another group of people opposite them on the cinema screen as well.

21

Jake watched the ink appear back into the pen.

Alf asked the bowlers to draw their favourite things or hobbies that they enjoyed doing in front of the audience.

The team opposite the bowlers were asked to do the same.

The bowlers worked out between them, discussing quietly that they were on a game show to win the pens.

They drew different things, with the audience laughing, talking, and pointing at their drawings on the big cinema screen in front of them.

Alf explained that they would win a pen each if their drawings were better than the opposition teams.

Ray and Robert both drew the Landfawcett bowling and ice-skating centre.

"Wow!" came from the audience.

Cara drew herself with sunglasses on a lounger on the sand by the sea with the sun in the sky.

Darren drew a book that he would like to read called Sexy Shenanigans with four sexy short stories in the same book.

Chris drew a gun with oil coming out of it that he had thought of earlier.

Philip drew himself with a butterfly.

Many strange things were drawn.

The bowlers got more claps, and wows than the opposition team.

The bowlers looked at Alf with a disgusted look with them feeling uneasy whispering to each other what a waste of time the game was to just win a pen each.

All of the items that they had drawn on the paper started to come alive out of the paper, appearing in front of them.

The bowlers stepped back like they were frightened with their jaws dropping at what they were seeing, talking about how shocked they were among themselves how this could happen.

Alf asked both teams to enter inside of their drawing to pick an item, or a piece out of their drawing for Alf and the audience to decide which team should win.

They picked each item up out of the paper, with it enlarging to the correct size needed automatically.

Everybody looked astonished at what they were seeing.

The audience voted for it to be a draw because both teams' drawings were different and really fantastic, this is what they could hear people saying in the audience.

Alf asked each team to enter a drawing of their choice, to choose which the audience would like the most with it being a draw.

They walked into Cara's drawing, relaxing on the beach in the sun.

The opposition team were making a snowman, it looked fresh, with the sparkling of the snow glistening.

The bowlers got the most votes winning a pen each, with the audience shouting. "Congratulations." And clapping loudly.

The bowlers bowed to thank them.

Popcorn was thrown at the opposition team.

Just as they were about to put their pens into their pockets Alf asked them to press the delete button at the side of their pens, the ink immediately drew back into the pens, with all of the items disappearing into the pens.

The audience left the room.

Darren whispered to his friends saying that it was probably going to be another very handy tool that would come in use to fight against the Windowir's, Vord, and Tiger.

Alf explained that inside each pen there was a wig with bullets inside of each tiny hair of the wig, the bullets automatically reload, only when on your heads.

The bowlers thanked Alf for the wig bullet pens that they had won.

Alf carried on explaining to press the button at the top of the pen once to release the wig, and a small yellow button saying shoot then appears, they then point the pen at what they want to kill and then press the yellow button, then the wig shoots at what the pen is pointing at, squeeze the pen after pressing the yellow button to shoot everything around you at the same time, press the button at the top of the pen again, then the wig goes back into the pen.

Harry commented. "This place is challenging, amazing and strange!"

They thanked Alf again for the pens, putting them into their pockets.

They carried on walking, noticing a sign on a door saying Relax, they walked into the room.

As they walked into what they thought was a room, it was not a room at all.

They suddenly fell into a deep hole, eventually landing into a large net tumbling into a heap, landing at the side of each other feeling squashed, and battered by the net cutting into their skin, and getting caught around their arms, and legs noticing that they were at ground level.

They noticed that the newspaper shop was at the side of the net that they were trapped inside of.

Jay drew a sharp knife with his pen; he used the knife to cut them out of the net, then pressed the delete button at the side of the pen, with the ink ejecting back into his pen, as they climbed out of the net, they said that they missed their older selves.

There was a shifty-looking gang of people with different needle bullets and guns in their hands, it looked like they were going to use them.

The bowlers stood outside of a newspaper shop watching the people with the guns for a while in case they started shooting.

Jake drew a large round barrier shield with his pen to protect them just in case they started shooting, no bullets were fired, so Jake deleted his barrier drawing.

The bowlers walked into the newspaper shop to ask the shopkeeper if he had seen the Windowir's outside before, with them not coming through a bright doorway.

Harry immediately thought that there was something not right with the person behind the counter; he looked fidgety with his hands like he had got something to hide.

Robert pointed to his head and mimed that he had no hat on to the other bowlers.

Jay whispered that the hat must have gone to blend in to look normal.

Jake whispered saying that he could be the leader in charge of them all.

Eric distracted the man, asking for some beans that he could not find pretending to be blind.

Chris and Charlie sneaked behind the counter looking for any guns.

Charlie noticed a pile of needle bullets with a gun at the side of him on a shelf.

Rex and Bruno ran around tripping the man up, the man was making a grab for the gun, just stroking the side of the gun on the way down to the floor with a bang.

Philip reached for the gun and the bullets, struggling to hold them.

Robert noticed and pointed out a dark blue shadow silhouette of themselves chasing behind them, the man picked up another gun that he had hidden on a hook under a shelf, and he started shooting at the bowlers as they rushed through the open door.

George shut the door sharply behind them, hoping to block the bullets from hitting them.

Chris panicked hearing the glass smash in the shop door, with bullets narrowly missing most of them.

Bullets sliced down one side of George and Robert's waist.

Darren noticed and pointed out to the rest of the bowlers that the shadows went through the middle of the shut shop door behind them.

Jay pointed out that the shadows were about to touch them.

The bowlers panicked running away faster out of breath with George, and Robert struggling to walk, with their pain in their waists making them feel like crying, hiding behind a large bin with George, and Robert looking like they were in even worse pain cradling their wounds with their hands, bending their bodies doubled over with pain.

They used their eye fingers to see what was going on, poking their eye fingers around the corner, the shadows and the backup gunners were searching for them.

George and Robert inspected their cuts; blood was running down their legs.

Eric put his arms around Penny tightly keeping her close, whispering goodbye to everybody, thinking that it was the end of their lives.

The shadows had found them, and they were about to touch them.

Paul covered his eyes, announcing that he felt scared.

The rings ejected tiny grains of dust from a star in each ring, the dust formed into a hand grabbing hold of the shadows following them, squeezing them until they had vanished, the star in each ring had filled ceasing to be visible, with only two stars remaining.

Jake noticed and pointed out that there were some backup gunners walking towards them, pointing their guns in front of them, about to shoot them.

Chris noticed that his blue smiley face on the bottom of his stick insect bottle had lit up, he then felt a trembling coming from it, with the top exploding off and hitting a gunner in the male reproduction system, a gale force wind blew the gunners away into the air, the jar suddenly shut like it was reloading itself, with the blue light on the bottle going back out.

Paul and Ben bumped into a lady with a tattoo on a tiny wrist bag that she was holding, knocking her flat onto her back onto the pavement with a pencil sharpener flying out of her hand to the other side of the road; they dashed past her, apologising to her, with her forgetting to pick the pencil sharpener up from the floor.

Darren picked her off the floor, noticing that the tattoo said Jargin on her tiny wrist bag.

Ray asked what Jargin meant.

She did not reply in a panic, explaining that she needed to carry on with her journey, noticing and pointing out George, and Robert's open bloody wounds, giving the bowlers a plaster for George, and Robert each from her pocket.

George and Robert thanked her.

She then walked off fast looking hurt rubbing her leg, and head together, while attempting to walk looking upset.

Robert and George pulled their black trousers down under their yellow shirts, then put a plaster on their wounds with them feeling better already.

Robert picked her pencil sharpener up from the ground and put it into his pocket.

Ray suggested following the lady to make sure that she was okay and to give the pencil sharpener back and see where she went to.

They followed her into a graffiti-filled alleyway that smelt disgusting, noticing that the injured lady from a distance had stood on an empty crisp bag on the floor; she then got sucked into the floor bag first, vanishing from sight, they noticed that the crisp bag was left behind on the floor in the same place.

The bowlers did the same as the lady, standing on the crisp bag with nothing happening, the bowlers looked puzzled hiding around the corner, they used their eye fingers one at a time, pointing at the crisp bag on the floor and recording all movement waiting for someone to appear.

Three hours went by, but nothing happened.

George and Robert's wounds felt a lot better; they were looking at their wounds, noticing that they were nearly completely healed already, commenting that the plasters must be made with magic.

Penny looked frightened, wondering what would happen next with a tear rolling down her face.

Eric gently wiped her tears away with his finger, kissing her and reassuring her that all would be okay.

Penny looked a little happier with a smile on her face.

They suddenly noticed a man appear from the crisp bag on Paul's phone through his eye finger camera, a sigh of relief came from all of the bowlers as the wait was finally over.

Cara suggested that they ran around the corner leading the way, with them hiding behind an oversized advertisement sign watching the man looking through Darren's eye finger camera on his phone screen, noticing that the man was looking around hoping that nobody had noticed him appear out of the crisp bag, his bag had a Jargin tattoo on it the same as the lady earlier.

The man walked the opposite way to the bowlers.

Jake and George walked fast behind the man; they caught him up, questioning him how he could appear out of a crisp bag.

The man looked shocked and lost for words, pulling a small yellow soft pencil sharpener that could be crunched into nothing out of his bag, the same as the pencil sharpener from the lady earlier in Robert's pocket.

The man explained that he was going to wipe their memories to half an hour before they had met him, explaining that it would not hurt and it was an invisible wave that changes time that appears out of the hole from the pencil sharpener, he held the pencil sharpener up at their faces about to press the button on the side.

Paul snatched the pencil sharpener from the man, stopping him.

Suddenly a group of Windowir's appeared behind them from the lit-up doorway that had appeared from nowhere.

Robert shouted. "Press and point your amnesia buttons at the Windowir's now!"

The bowlers pressed with the Windowir's immediately looking confused, like they had forgotten what they were doing.

The bowlers made sure that the coast was clear, they then ran into the launderette behind them, with the man that had appeared out of the crisp bag.

Cara explained what had happened, and how they had got there.

The man introduced himself, saying that his name was Leo, he quizzed the bowlers about where the whistles had come from, and where the tattoos on Cara, Ray and Philip had come from.

They explained the situation, and how they had got the whistles from Charlie's mum from the strange man from the market.

Leo suddenly announced that he would show them what he was doing, explaining that it was a secret place that he had come from, and that is why he was going to wipe their memories.

They crept out of the launderette, following Leo back into the alley where the crisp bag was.

Leo explained. "We need to hold hands in a line, and then my tattoo wrist bag key will open the crisp bag gate and let us enter inside!"

They held hands, and paws in a line entering the crisp bag gate.

On their journey through the time portal, Paul asked Leo if any crisp bag would let them enter inside.

Leo explained. "I have glued that particular crisp bag onto the floor for my convenience so that I do not have to carry it around, any crisp bag will transport us as it automatically connects to the tattoo bag when the tattoo is facing the crisp bag!"

They suddenly appeared in a room full of people with computers in front of them, sitting behind desks looking through closed-circuit television.

Leo explained that it was a secret undercover project to find ways to get hold of the Windowir's leaders called Tiger, and Vord to stop more people's lives been taken away from their families, and friends.

Paul asked Leo how they knew Tiger, and Vord's names, and how they knew that they were in control of the Windowir's.

Robert explained to Leo how he was puzzled about the man in the shop with no glass hat on earlier.

Leo explained. "Tiger was recorded on closed-circuit television stealing guns from the police, armed forces and people's homes, and that some long term experienced trusted Windowir's did blend in with no hats to make them look like normal people!"

Jay interrupted in a shocked tone of voice. "This is unbelievable!"

Leo carried on explaining that Tiger then turns the guns into needle bullet guns; they then shoot innocent people, turning them into his growing gang of Windowir's, people that were shot were then brain-dead; once their glass hats had appeared on to their heads, they were in a trance, and taken away through a bright white lit doorway portal to the planet Opack.

Penny commented. "It will be hard to find and kill them all!"

Philip was a little overwhelmed with a tear in his eye, feeling emotional but more determined to try to solve the problem of people being taken away.

Robert sat in deep thought with his hands on either side of his head, and his elbows on his knees, saying. "Did you hear about the actor that fell through the floorboards, he was just going through a stage?"

Charlie replied. "Very funny."

Leo explained that he and his team had followed Tiger undercover for a long time, and they were trying to track down a key that Tiger had kept mentioning from near to the planet Opack.

Darren mentioned in a hopeful tone of voice that the key may be able to set the Windowir's free.

22

The undercover reflectorglass eyes disguise.

Leo commented that his undercover people had kept their distance to keep themselves safe from the Windowir's, Tiger and Vord.

Ben mentioned that he felt scared for them and asked what Tiger looked like.

Leo explained that Tiger looked normal, but he just had got a larger glass hat on his head, and he was very tall.

Darren replied saying that they would notice him if he was in front of them, probably.

Leo said that he and his team repeatedly noticed that Tiger, the Windowir's, and Vord were removing the trees that had lost their leaves from being shot with the needle bullets and they were trying to find out where they were going.

Paul looked sad in the face at the trees and wildlife being affected.

Leo showed the bowlers his unique reflectorglass eyes that he loved.

The bowlers looked at Leo strangely, asking what he was talking about.

Leo explained that his undercover reflectorglass eyes were his disguise that looked like a pair of white flexible swimming goggles and they were made from a soft material until placed on the face, they then go translucent, then as you look into reflective material such as glass, or a mirror of the person that you want to turn into, that persons face from the reflection then appears onto your face making you a double of that person until you take the Reflectorglass eyes goggles off, then you go back to yourself immediately.

The bowlers discussed how handy this would be.

Leo explained how helpful they were to him.

Darren asked Leo what they would do with Tiger, and the Windowir's if and when they do catch them with them being so dangerous.

Leo explained that there was a team of talking robots, one was called Zon with a human-programmed brain that looks and acts like a real person that recognises and shoots back at Tiger, the Windowir's, and Vord.

Ray mentioned how he would love to meet Tiger and shoot him dead.

The bowlers explained that they had met Zon earlier with him pushing them down the slide and taking them away from danger.

Leo explained that Tiger was in the next village called Bow yesterday, taking people away through a brightly lit door.

Zon and his team were trying to track and follow Tiger and the Windowir's.

Cara commented. "It must be Zon's robot team that is protecting us from death!"

Jake asked if they could have a pair of reflectorglass eyes for each of them, they looked at the glasses, noticing that they could be scrunched into a small ball so that they could easily fit into their whistle pouches with their hats.

Philip spoke. "I lost my glasses the other day, I said out loud whoever has stolen my glasses I have got contacts!"

Robert replied. "That is funny."

Chris described the tools that they had on their whistles, pointing out his favourite item: the magical shower cap to make them small or, turn them into anything that they think of.

Harry commented. "I like his whistle with it saying Emily on repeat, I am reminiscing about our last adventure; I am curious what other things the oil and glass buttons do?"

Robert mentioned. "The smart flowers powers with the force field protects us!"

Jake mentioned. "Our pens and pocket watches that only we can use to get rid of Tiger, Vord, and the Windowir's are so cool!"

Chris spoke. "What time is it?"

Jake laughed. "Time that you got a watch!"

Chris replied. "Very funny."

Leo immediately gave them a pair each of reflectorglass eye goggles, they put them into their whistle compartments with their hats.

Philip asked if they could also have a few tattoo wrist bags to get in and out of the crisp bag gate.

Leo gave Chris a tattoo wrist bag, explaining. "You only need one to re-enter, when you are all holding hands and tails!"

They thanked Leo.

Leo explained that if they pressed the silver button on the bag when it was not in use, it would turn into a small silver flower petal, with the button ready to turn back into a bag as needed when pressed again.

Jake put the silver petal into his whistle compartment with his shower hat.

Leo heard the bowlers talking about Chris's whistle, and how nice it sounded, with all of the lovely noises from the leaves crunching.

Leo was curious to hear Chris's whistle, asking Chris to blow his whistle just before they left.

Chris blew his whistle, and Leo loved the whistles leaf-crunching noises.

Jake pressed the silver button releasing the tattoo bag pointing it at the ceiling, transporting them back up out of the crisp bag, back into the disgusting alley, with them carrying on their journey holding hands, flying on to Bow City to investigate more, they suddenly flew into a large net getting tangled in it, then fell and landed into a net below.

A few ladies were watching them in horror at what they were seeing while enjoying a drink, the ladies did not know what to do to help in a panic, asking if they could help.

The bowlers were trapped and unable to move, asking the ladies to try to break the net.

Philip panicked the most, trying to get out with no success, with the ropes suddenly turning into snakes biting them, they were watching the orange poison entering their veins in their bodies, with them feeling powerless to help themselves.

The ladies apologised because they had nothing available to break the net, and they were just stood looking distressed, discussing that they could go to find help.

The bowlers shouted that any help would be great.

Eric commented. "It is like being stuck in the middle of a snakes wedding!"

Harry shouted pen, they pressed their pen tops, and yellow buttons releasing their wigs, placing them onto their heads, pointing, and shooting at the snakes.

Cara and Tom panicked the most for their lives, trying not to fall asleep heavy-eyed, with poison entering into their bodies.

Jay opened his pocket watch, releasing the go-carts, breaking the net under them with the weight releasing them.

The ladies looked happier that the snakes were dead, and they had got out of the net.

Robert and Charlie were the only ones who were not bitten and falling asleep, they suddenly landed on to a large kid's bouncy castle full of silver dust; the bounciness automatically sent them up and down into the air, until they landed stationery, the sparkly silver dust covered the group of friends from head to foot, the silver dust entered into the wounds of those been bitten, silver poison ejected from their wounds.

Robert and Charlie also got covered in the sparkly silver poisonous dust from head to foot, as it had left their wounds, the bowlers that were bitten started to wake hysterically thinking that the snakes were still on them, a little bit of silver dust and blood was trickling out from the areas where they had been bitten, they calmed down noticing that the dead snakes were at the side of them on the floor, they felt unclean from the silver dust ejecting onto them.

The wigs entered back into the pens automatically.

The ladies who had seen what had happened gave them a box of tissues to mop up the blood, and the silver poison, the tissue box had a rainbow-coloured button at the side of it saying. 'Press me.'

Harry looked at the rainbow button pressing it, but he suddenly vanished from sight, they looked for Harry, thinking not again.

Both ladies looked shocked at what they had just seen happen.

Darren noticed that Paul had picked the tissue box up, inspecting it and watching him.

Robert commented. "I really need a shower!"

Darren could not believe his eyes, noticing that Paul had knocked the rainbow button as well, with him vanishing also, they decided that nobody else should touch the tissue box, or press the rainbow button, or they would pass from sight the same as Harry and Paul.

Philip threw the tissue box away from them, not looking very happy; it landed at the side of the ladies who gave them the tissue box, as the bowlers walked off both ladies ran after them shouting for the bowlers to come back, they arrived back with the ladies, the ladies explained that they had heard voices coming out of the tissue box, with a conversation with Harry and Paul asking each other why it was dark.

Tom questioned Harry and Paul where they were through his blue talk button on his whistle.

Tom had a faint reply saying that they were in blackness, and they did not know where they were, but they felt injured from what felt like an earthquake.

Cara laughed to herself, asking everybody to carry on, thinking that the ladies were hearing things.

A lady explained that their earthquake would have been the box being thrown, as they slowly walked back shouting Harry and Paul loudly, they had a silent pause to listen in between, and they heard a faint reply saying that they were in the dark coming from the tissue box, one of the ladies walked up to Philip and gave him the tissue box.

Philip spoke. "I am just thinking that anybody that sneezes without a tissue takes matters into their own hands!"

The bowlers pulled a strange face, laughing.

Rex and Bruno looked tired of walking, looking a little bit out of breath slowing down.

Philip thanked the lady for the tissue box, then carried the tissue box apologising for throwing the tissue box, not realising that they were inside, walking and talking to Harry and Paul stuck inside of the tissue box on their way to the City of Bow.

The bowlers discussed that Tiger must have caused Harry and Paul to cease to be visible, and all of a sudden, a lit-up door appeared in front of them.

A gang of Windowir's appeared out of nowhere shouting, "Say goodbye to your life as you know it, and you will all join us now!"

Chris drew an oil gun and then shot the Windowir's covering them in oil, the Windowir's started sliding about on the oil under their feet while attempting to point and shoot their guns at everybody, the bowlers laughed to themselves at the Windowir's nearly falling while shooting and missing them.

Harry and Paul suddenly got louder shouting, "Thank you Zon for shouting shower cap through our whistles on repeat!"

Cara's dart jar had a lit-up blue smiley face on the bottom with it shaking erratically like it was going to explode full of red darts.

Harry and Paul outgrew the tissue box with it shredding like confetti, they appeared back to their normal size in front of Cara, with their magical shower caps on, they looked relieved to be back to their normal size, commenting how claustrophobic they had felt inside of the tissue box.

Cara commented. "We need something else good to happen with bad things happening like a shower to appear out of nowhere so that we can get clean!"

Harry and Paul put their magical shower caps away in their whistles, trying not to get shot dodging the bullets and laughing.

Cara's jar blue smiley face lit up that was attached to the stick insect containing the red darts inside, it suddenly burst open releasing the red darts; the red darts stabbed every Windowir in their necks, making them fall to their death, two darts changed colour from red to yellow in mid-air, hitting Harry and Paul, just as they had grown tall from the box in the way of the darts.

Harry and Paul had a yellow dart that had entered into the side of their necks, making them fall unconscious to the floor.

The blue smiley face on Cara's jar went back to normal with the top going back onto the jar slightly.

The bowlers looked devastated, noticing Harry and Paul on the floor trying to bring them around, tapping them with no response, then darts reappeared back in Cara's jar, with the jar shutting and sealing properly, with no light.

The bowlers ran away from the Windowir's struggling to drag Harry and Paul along on the floor, with them talking about them sadly that they had been in the wrong place at the wrong time.

Charlie announced that he had noticed the sign saying. 'City of Bow.'

Robert pointed at a crisp bag on the floor, shouting. "Run over to that crisp bag as fast as you all can with me, it is obviously our entrance to Leo!"

23

The tattoo bag had changed from Bow to Jargin.

Jake removed the petal from his whistle, pressing the silver button to release the tattoo bag.

They used the tattoo bag holding hands to transport them into the room of safety, with Tom entering the crisp bag first with them meeting Leo again.

Eric noticed and pointed out that the tattoo name on the bag had changed, saying Bow on it, instead of Jargin.

Ray pressed the silver button on the bag turning it back into a silver petal and put it into his pocket, they explained to Leo that they could not work out why Harry and Paul had got a yellow dart, instead of a red dart in their neck, but they were still breathing but unconscious.

Leo suggested that it could be Tiger causing trouble, and he must have placed the tissue box as a trap that went wrong for him.

They guessed that Zon must have somehow changed Harry and Paul's darts yellow to make them stay alive, but unconscious, instead of being dead.

Leo looked back through the closed-circuit television, watching the darts change from red to yellow just before they hit Harry and Paul, bringing a tear to their eyes.

Chris started to take some photos on his eye finger camera of Harry and Paul getting hit by the darts from the closed-circuit television.

Leo explained. "Myself, Zon and the rest of my team are still trying to catch Tiger and the Windowir's, Tiger's, evil team of Windowir's are fighting against Zon's good team, like a tug of war, between good, and bad things happening sometimes, Zon helps us all against evil as much as he can!"

Tom looked shocked. "We need to help to sort all of this mess out!"

Paul and Harry looked dead, but they were still alive with their chests moving up and down, and their air was blowing from their mouths.

Ray pressed the silver button, releasing the tattoo bag out of the silver petal.

The bowlers held hands and re-entered Bow City with the tattoo bag in George's hand.

Ray pressed the silver button on the bag to turn it back into a silver petal, then gave the petal to Robert for him to save it.

Tom suggested. "Let's leave Paul and Harry on the side of a shop door with them being unconscious."

Philip looked tearful, with everybody else joining in feeling sad that Harry and Paul had no response when spoken to, or movement from them apart from breathing.

The blue smiley face at the end of Charlie's jar lit up on his chest attached to the stick insect with it popping open, making Harry and Paul hover in the air, following behind the bowlers.

Charlie's blue smiley face then went back to normal with the jar top appearing back on.

Harry and Paul were hovering over Rex and Bruno with the dogs circling below them with them making a whimpering noise like they knew that there was something wrong.

There were crowds of people walking around them, rubbernecking and staring at Harry and Paul.

A large group of Windowir's ran towards them from a brightly lit doorway that had stayed open shining brightly.

The bowlers pressed at the side of their pens, releasing their wigs with them putting them onto their heads shooting the Windowir's.

Robert drew a large screen to protect them.

The Windowir's shot at the bowlers.

The bowlers shot back with their pen wigs, mainly from behind the screen, dodging the bullets, making them hit innocent strangers behind them.

Darren drew a gun, shooting it at the Windowir's.

Charlie opened his pocket watch, releasing money like it was rain.

Jay poked a Windowir in the eye with his finger, distracting him.

The bowlers picked the coins up and threw them at the Windowir while still avoiding the glass bullets hurdling towards them.

People who were hit by the bullets had spider web-forming glass hats on their heads while in a trance following the Windowir leader.

The injured lead Windowir gave the last person in the line his gun to shoot and kill, while still on the way into the large brightly lit doorway.

People quickly crowded around looking scared, collecting the money, and throwing it at the Windowir's from behind a large screen that Robert had drawn with his pen.

George grabbed hold of a newly formed Windowir at the back of the line holding the gun, entering into the brightly lit doorway, and was fighting with him to pull the gun from him.

Jay immobilised him to the floor, drawing handcuffs around his wrists with his pen.

As Charlie shut his pocket watch, they watched the money that was about to fall out of the pocket watch enter back inside.

Jake's blue smiley face on his jar lit up stuck to the stick insect, with the bottle lid suddenly popping off, releasing a rope tying the Windowir's hands up automatically.

Jay pressed the delete button at the top of the pen, and the button at the side of the pen making the ink re-enter inside.

Charlie's blue smiley face lit up, making the Windowir join Harry and Paul in the air.

Charlie's blue smiley face went back to normal with the jar lid shutting.

The Windowir had an evil look, shouting for them to let him go.

Rex and Bruno were below them.

Philip looked upset with his younger grandad Paul hovering behind them, still unconscious.

People glared at them in shock at what they had just seen.

They walked along and noticed that there was a large translucent, glowing bubble ahead with seats inside for them to sit down on, as the bowlers walked closer to the bubble, they noticed their names were written on the outside of the glass in organised and shaped water droplets, it was bobbing about on the water with the door open.

The bowlers cautiously entered the doorway, sitting down on the seats provided.

Harry, Paul and the Windowir hovered in the air in the middle of them, they were not sure if they were doing the right thing not knowing what to expect as they entered, the bubble door shut and then set off fast, they held onto their seats with Paul, Harry and the Windowir randomly jerking about in the middle of them.

The Windowir attempted to set himself free with no joy.

They travelled under the water watching the bubbles flow up to the top from the fish breathing, and moving around, and chatting about the situation, feeling like they had been inside of the bubble for a long time.

Philip spoke. "The bubble is slowing down."

The bowlers noticed a shipwreck ahead of them with them coming to a stop at the bottom of the ocean, their rings suddenly had a yellow light on them, with an oxygen-breathing mask appearing on their faces helping them to breathe including the Windowir, the dogs, and unconscious Harry and Paul.

The bubble door opened with them leaving the bubble noticing a large strange blue building with strange large bubble-shaped windows under the water, swimming along looking around for a doorway with Cara, Philip and Ray, pushing Harry, Paul, and the Windowir along with them, entering inside of a plain white door, with water gently ejecting out of the door leaving them and the room water free inside, they felt like they should be able to breathe, so they moved their breathing masks above their eyes up onto their heads.

Cara found a book on a table with writing on the front page.

Robert read the writing. "The Windowir's, Tiger, and Vord need their black guns to form their team!"

Robert looked puzzled. "That is a strange book!"

Philip picked up the book, trying to open it up, soon realising that there was a padlock that was locked, stopping him from opening it.

Robert commented. "It must be a secret place hidden away from Tiger, Vord, and the Windowir's!"

Zon appeared from nowhere and stood looking at the bowlers, explaining that they needed to get the key from planet Opack which was a billion light years away, and they needed to open the padlock on the side of the book so that they could find out what was inside and hopefully get rid of Tiger, the Windowirs and Vord to save the world, and he advised them to do what they could to get the key.

Cara gave Ray a hair clip for him to attempt to pick the lock.

Ray asked Zon where the key was and what the book did.

Darren spoke. "It is like we are in some kind of dream!"

Ray was trying to pick the lock on the padlock with a hair clip that Cara had given him, the padlock threw out a strong wind throwing Ray to the floor.

Cara asked Ray. "Are you okay?"

Ray stood up dazed after banging his head on the floor.

Zon replied. "I have tracked the key to the book with my special key tracker, the key is on planet Opack, and I would love to open the book myself; my guess is that the key has caused the Windowir's to exist!"

Darren asked Zon how he had tracked the key with the key tracker.

Zon explained. "As soon as the book and the key appeared a few years ago, I thought that it looked suspicious with what was written on it, so I invented a key tracker putting my tracker on the key, only noticing that it had vanished a few months ago!"

Jake commented. "We do not know how to get to Opack, or what to do to get the key back!"

Zon explained. "I will help you the best that I can, while also helping normal people!"

Rex and Bruno were staring at Harry and Paul, looking sad at them hovering.

Zon gave the bowlers his small bead key tracker, leaving them to it.

Jake put the small bead tracker into his whistle compartment.

Paul remarked. "It reminds me of Rex's whistle bead noise!"

The bowlers asked Zon how they would know if they were near to the key.

Zon explained that the bead had tiny writing on it, saying the location of the key so that they have an idea of the location.

George suggested. "I hope that Tom's reading glass jar will open so that we can see the writing when needed!"

They thanked Zon, hoping that their eyes were good enough to see the location if the glasses jar did not open.

Zon went to help other people again, vanishing from sight.

They walked down some pink glittery steps noticing a room saying oil space bowling on the front; they were intrigued walking in, noticing transparent balls full of oil, the oil inside of the transparent space bowling balls were swishing about inside as they rolled along the floor.

The bowlers decided that they would play a game of oil space bowling against the group of teenagers that lived there.

They started to play the competitive game with the bowlers winning the game, finally after plenty of fun and laughter playing it.

The teenagers put some music on pouring alcoholic Blue Rock Cool into drinking glasses drinking plenty of Blue Rock Cool, making them feel very happy and talking loudly, and ate the chicken wraps provided and chilled out

listening to music for a few hours
having a few more drinks.

The teenagers gave the bowlers an
oil bowling ball each, explaining that it
shrinks to the size of a small coin when
touched where the rainbow button was
on the top pressing the rainbow button
on their oil ball shrinking the oil balls to
the size of a small coin.

The bowlers commented and
discussed how amazing the oil balls
were, being able to shrink them to such
a small size, then they started to explain
to the teenagers about the tissue box
rainbow button, and what it had done
to Harry and Paul while putting their
coins into their whistle pouches.

The teenagers said that they would
help by looking after the unconscious
three.

George thanked them.

The bowlers drank too much Blue Rock Cool dropping asleep for a while.

Penny and Eric slept with their arm around each other to keep close, cuddling one another.

They slowly woke after a good sleep.

Unconscious Harry, Paul, and the Windowir stayed with the teenagers, with the bowlers thanking the teenagers for their help, then they re-entered the glowing bubble and travelled back to Bow City for more clues.

Penny smiled, commenting while travelling. "This Blue Rock Cool drink is lovely!"

Suddenly water bubbles started dancing around on the outside of the glowing bubble that they were enclosed inside, the bubbles formed a picture of a key with a virtual gun shape above the key shooting towards them with it turning red as blood as it splattered on to the glowing glass, they arrived with the door opening, they stepped out of the large plastic glowing bubble, there was a door shaped light that had appeared in front of them, with a small group of Windowir's shooting at them.

24

The virtual key on the outside of the bubble room!

Rex and Bruno ran at the Windowir's making them fall to the floor.

All Robert could talk about was the virtual key on the outside of the bubble room that they had travelled in, in between trying not to get shot.

Philip's jar suddenly had a blue smiley face that had lit up, with the jar opening covering the Windowir's with mini-brain, the blue smiley face went back to normal with the lid going back onto the jar nearly, and more brain appeared back inside of the jar making it go back to normal and shutting properly with it being full again.

Robert spoke. "I am astonished how the jars can do that!"

The brain soaked into the Windowir's skin making them suddenly change from no expression on their faces to a puzzled expression wondering where they were, the Windowir's suddenly woke up properly from their walking brainless sleep running off to find their families.

Charlie suggested. "The key made of bubbles must be a clue of some sort on how to collect the key from the planet Opack!"

Jake removed the bead from his whistle, looking at the writing on the bead and finding out where the key was, the writing was too small to read, so he put it back away inside of his whistle pouch.

Tom's blue smiley face lit up on his jar with his reading glasses popping out, Jake got the bead back out of his pouch using the reading glasses to look through them, noticing that it said unknown where the key was, but it was thirteen, point nine trillion miles away.

The bowlers looked puzzled, with Tom's jar going back to normal with glasses appearing back inside, with the top appearing back on the top of the jar.

Jake put the bead back into his pouch.

They discussed how puzzling it was that the key was in an unknown place.

Robert suggested that the key must be in, or near to water.

Philip disagreed because the key would go rusty in water.

Jay shared his thoughts, thinking that it was a warning for them to back off as well as a clue, with the virtual gun shooting towards them, and blood-coloured water appearing.

Darren suggested giving in and going back to their year twenty-twenty-five before they all die and there is no future for any of them.

Ray shouted that they needed to carry on for all of their sakes, and others to attempt to have a normal life.

They all agreed with Ray.

Penny and Eric cuddled, saying that they wanted to be together forever.

Tom noticed a small group of Windowir's appearing from a brightly lit doorway, a baby blanket from a pram flew up into the air, with a strong force of wind out of nowhere covering a Windowir.

The bowlers pressed the rainbow button on their coins opening up their oil bowling balls, with them throwing the balls at the Windowir's, some oil balls got shot by the Windowir's releasing the inside solution realising that it was definitely oil with the oily feel of it, the oil from inside of the balls went all over the Windowir's bodies missing one Windowir, as the oil touched the Windowir's they started to change back to normal people.

The ex Windowir's were asking where their relatives, and friends were.

The Windowir that missed being hit by the oil shot Jake with a glass hat appearing on Jake's head, the Windowir retreated back through the lit doorway, taking Jake with him.

The bowlers realised and discussed that they needed to go to get more oil bowling balls to cure everybody.

The ex Windowir's muttered about a large brown dragon that was vegetarian called Vord on the planet Opack that eats the trees and leaves that were brought from earth, in-between breathing fire.

The bowlers then worked out and realised that the trees were most probably being taken away for dragon Vord to eat.

The bowlers flew through the air back to the glowing bubble on the water, as they arrived the bubble door was open, they entered into the bubble, and then travelled back to the shipwreck, as they arrived the door opened, and they stepped out of the bubble, the bowlers entered the white door with the teenagers stood in front of them.

Ray spoke. "Do you know why the shipwrecked pirates got cakes and cookies when they got washed up?"

Robert replied. "Please tell us why?"

Ray replied. "Because it was a deserted island!"

Jake replied. "Very funny."

The teenagers welcomed them back; they enjoyed a drink of Blue Rock Cool together.

Cara asked the teenagers for more oil bowling ball coins, as this and Philip's brain jar were the cure.

The teenagers gave the bowlers all of the ball coins that they had, the teenagers jokingly said that if the bowlers needed any more ball coins, they needed to go back in time to twenty years ago to Bow City when there were more being made.

The bowlers walked back to the glowing bubble with the teenagers, the bubble door was open, and they thanked the teenagers for their help in looking after the three of them, they then took Harry, Paul, and the Windowir back into the bubble with them.

Robert commented. "I hope that Jake cooperates with the Windowir!"

Ray commented. "Jake has got no choice but to cooperate with the Windowir!"

The bowlers arrived back at Bow City leaving the bubble, discussing going back in time twenty years to get more oil balls from when they were making them in the factory.

They turned their dial to two-thousand and four and pressed their yellow buttons holding hands with Cara, Philip, Penny, and Ray, they got transported through time back to Bow

City in two-thousand and four through their whistles noticing a poster with two-thousand and four written on it.

Charlie spoke. "I am not sure where we should go or look first!"

Darren pointed out a pub over the road from them, saying that he could do with a drink.

A group of friends that were sitting on a bench outside of the pub in the sun were talking loudly among themselves mentioning the bowlers and their names not realising that they were behind them, they looked amazed at a 3D map pressing the star on the map together laughing with nothing happening.

Robert walked up to them and asked them where the oil bowling ball factory was.

Darren suddenly noticed his mum Wendy sitting on the bench, whispering his strange news to his bowler friends.

The bowlers looked at Wendy, noticing that she was young in the face, and the same as old photos at home in twenty-twenty-five.

Wendy's friends glared at them, talking about the bowlers, deciding if they were the correct people speaking in a lower tone of voice.

Wendy questioned. "What are your names?"

As they said their names, Wendy looked positive with her eyes lighting up like a light bulb, and a smile giving them the 3D map.

The bowlers thought that the 3D map looked very interesting, with lots of detail, asking Wendy why she had given them the map.

Wendy explained that a lady had knocked on her front door saying that the bowlers would find her putting the map in her hands, explaining that the raised star helps them travel through time, explaining that she had attempted to give her the map back, but she had walked off faster than you could blink.

Wendy and her friends explained that they did not know how to get to the oil bowling ball factory, apologising.

Darren noticed a glint in his younger mum's eye, knowing that, that glint would be him one day.

Wendy said goodbye, then walked back to her friends.

Darren shouted. "See you in a few years, Mum." With a happy tear in his eye.

Wendy looked back, obviously wondering what Darren was talking about.

Jake held the 3D map with them all stood looking at it.

Robert asked everybody to press the star button, mentioning to think of the factory.

The bowlers then got transported through time, they were stood looking up at how big the bowling ball factory was in front of them, as they walked inside there were wheelbarrows full of oil ball coins being made by the factory people, the bowlers asked if they could have a wheelbarrow full of coins each to take away to save the world for free.

The workers just laughed and walked away, calling the bowlers cheeky for asking.

The bowlers heard the workers while walking away in the opposite direction, they were discussing if they should ask if any were going to be thrown away while walking back inside, and they asked the workers very nicely if there were any wheelbarrows full of coins that were being thrown away that they could take away with them?

Chris spoke. "The other day the beekeepers gave me thirteen bees when I only asked for twelve, I said Hey you gave me one too many, he replied with, that's a freebie."

Charlie laughed, setting everyone else off.

25

The Magical Rings Flashed Pink!

The workers refused to let them have any coins because they recycled all of the rejected coins.

The bowlers walked outside to discuss what to do next.

The rings started to flash pink on their fingers, including Penny's tattoo ring.

Chris mentioned about the pink light from the rings appearing when they swapped memories, and thoughts, realising this could happen again now if they wanted.

Tom found it interesting how the rings connected in different ways, like they were suggesting that option to attempt to confuse the factory workers with them lighting up.

Philip suggested to each person to grab a wheelbarrow full of coins each, then to transport twenty years forward into the future through time holding hands, they agreed walking back into the factory, they suddenly all looked confused, swapping thoughts and memories with each other distracting the factory workers slightly.

The workers did not know what was going on, because the bowlers looked confused, the workers suddenly grabbed hold of the bowlers and then threw them out of the building.

The bowlers were disappointed that their plan did not work still feeling a little confused.

Ray suggested for someone to put on the reflectorglass eyes and turn into a worker to smuggle a wheelbarrow full of ball coins out of the factory.

Darren got his pair of reflectorglass eyes out of his whistle compartment ready.

A lady walked out of the factory past lots of windows.

Darren passed his pair of reflectorglass eyes to Cara, with her putting them on like a pair of swimming goggles, with them going translucent on her face, she then looked at the ladies reflection in the glass window.

Cara turned into the lady that she had looked at through the reflectorglass eyes walking into the factory and wheeled a wheelbarrow full of oil ball coins out of the factory.

A factory worker man kept shouting Alice directly behind Cara.

Cara realised that he was thinking that Cara was Alice.

Cara said nothing and just looked behind her and carried on walking away faster.

The worker chased Cara, asking where she was taking the wheelbarrow full of coins.

The bowlers noticed that Cara was on her way back to them being chased.

Jake opened his pocket watch with them all boarding the helicopter that had appeared from Jake's pocket watch, and Cara wheeled the wheelbarrow onto the helicopter last, with them flying away together as fast as they could.

Cara removed the reflecorglass eyes, giving them back to Darren with her face turning back to normal, with Darren putting the reflectorglass eyes back into his whistle pouch.

Cara explained how frightened and nervous she felt being followed.

They thought that there would still not be enough oil ball coins, they landed on the ground away from the factory.

Jake shut his pocket watch, and they watched the helicopter disappear back inside again.

They pressed their yellow buttons and turned their dials to twenty-twenty-four, holding hands, transporting twenty years through time in front immediately, back to the year twenty-twenty-four.

Philip looked and sounded happy that they could now cure Harry, and Paul with the oil from the ball coins to make them normal again.

The bowlers noticed a gang of Windowir's walking towards them, they held an oil ball each ready, pressing the top of their pens to release their wigs, then put them on their heads pressing their yellow buttons to shoot at the Windowir's.

The Windowir's started shooting back at them.

Each oil ball that got shot immediately burst open onto the floor.

They were not close enough to the Windowir's, so it made no difference with none of the oil touching the Windowir's, some of the Windowir's were dead from the wig bullets.

Cara and Robert got shot in the leg by the Windowir's, with the bullets forming a glass hat on their heads, making them follow the lead shooter.

Philip wheeled his wheelbarrow over to the Windowir's, Cara and Robert, just as they were about to enter the brightly lit doorway, Philip felt really helpful throwing the oil onto the Windowir's Cara, and Robert, curing them with satisfaction and a big smile.

Philip got shot several times while pouring and throwing the oil at the

Windowir's, noticing them change to good people again, while a glass hat formed on Philip's head turning him into a Windowir.

The bowlers were hurt but still managed to pour oil over Philip to cure him, then they discussed how they needed to go to treat Harry, and Paul with the oil balls that were left over, and were not damaged, and discussed how they had no idea how to get to the planet Opack to go to try to find the key to open the book.

Philip suggested that they pressed the star, with them pressing the star on the 3D map, thinking about the bubble, they watched the world flash by fast in a quarter of a second travelling through different places in time back to the bubble, as they arrived they entered the open door, travelling down back to the shipwreck, as they left the bubble the teenagers welcomed them.

Charlie announced how they were happy to be back.

The teenagers took the bowlers to Harry, Paul, and the Windowir, they were happy to be back with the teenagers and started to puncture the oil balls with a sharp stick from the floor, they then poured oil over Harry, Paul, and the Windowir curing them making them go back to normal, they were overjoyed to be a team once again re-entering the bubble, sat together, chatting amongst one another.

Harry, Paul, and the Windowir had so many questions on the way back to the city of Bow.

Chris realised that there were only a few oil ball coins left sharing his bad news.

The bowlers discussed what to do next, panicking that there were not enough to save everybody, as they arrived back the door opened and they walked out noticing the sign saying, 'Bow City.'

The bowlers were happy to be back together, patting each other on the shoulder; they then hugged each other.

Darren and Robert pointed out a crisp bag on the floor saying that it could be a hint for them to use it, in a panic, Paul mentioned to Chris to use the tattoo wrist bag.

Robert gave Chris the petal for him to have a go.

Chris touched the silver button on the petal to make it go back to its normal size.

Robert noticed and pointed out that it said Bow City on the tattoo bag.

The bowlers held hands, and tails with Chris re-entering through the crisp bag first.

As soon as the bowlers had arrived, they asked Leo if he had any ideas.

Chris then pressed the silver button, putting the petal back into his pocket.

Leo welcomed them looking through the closed-circuit television together looking for anything strange, suggesting using the raised star on the 3D map to enter into the planet Opack if it was on the map to get the key, the bowlers looked at every inch of the 3D map; they were not surprised that there was no sign of planet Opack on the map because that would be too easy.

Leo said. "Zon must have handed Wendy the 3D map for you to use!"

Paul and Harry both suggested that this must be a second clue on the map to get to planet Opack.

Jay turned the 3D map over to look at the underside to see if there was anything that would help them.

Penny noticed a key shape pointing it out.

Jay tried to rip the key from the map with his hand going straight through the key, with the key reflecting onto his hand, the fake 3D water moved around gently covering the key, swishing around with 3D water droplets splashing into the air.

Penny tried to touch and catch the water droplets with no water to touch; the droplets reflected back onto Penny's hands as well.

The bowlers looked in astonishment, discussing how strange this was.

Eric put his arm around Penny's lower back to stay close, giving her a gentle squeeze and sharing a tender kiss.

The rest of the bowlers smiled, looking happy for them.

George suggested pressing the water button on their whistles, they held their whistles with one hand pressing their water buttons and used their other hand to connect their spare hands with one on top of one another, touching the key on the 3D map, they suddenly got transported through different worlds, they guessed that they were on their way to planet Opack feeling apprehensive.

Jake shouted to Zon on their way in case they needed help.

They unexpectedly stopped in the middle of nowhere with them stuck, hovering in the air about to fall to their death, falling to the ground.

Charlie grabbed hold of Philip's hand, shouting. "Hold hands and use your whistles to fly to live, or you will die."

Eric had hold of Penny and Cara's hands, blowing his whistle while struggling to push his own black button with them flying along.

George held Ray's hands and touched his black button and blew his whistle, flying to the rest of the bowlers, with them listening to the ridiculous whistle noises mashed together.

Jake and Paul made sure that Rex and Bruno had their whistles next to their mouths, forming a group with them having a discussion about what to do next.

Ray, Cara, Philip, and Penny did most of the talking with no good outcome results.

Tom commented saying that Zon must have stopped them halfway, thinking that they were in need of help.

Cara and Penny started to cry, panicking that they were going to be stuck there forever.

They all had utter panic written on their faces, with everyone trying to calm Cara and Penny with no joy.

A tall man with a large flashing blue glass hat appeared out of nowhere through a brightly lit doorway floating in the air at the side of them, the man connected to the rings, making them flash blue.

26

The trees are being killed for Dragon Vord on planet Opack.

The hat opened up with a hole at the top of it sucking the bowler gang into the air and pulling them into the hat feet first one at a time, as they had arrived inside of the hat, they were in a prison full of trees and Windowir's.

A lady stood in front of them introducing herself as Miana with an evil laugh, she demanded that they either turn into Windowir's, or they will die, explaining that they were killing the trees on earth temporarily so that they were more manageable to transport them to the planet Opack with fewer leaves, and Opack needs the trees more than the earth because Opack was dying from the lack of fresh air, and benefiting herself feeding dragon Vord, and the Windowir's with the fruits that grow.

The bowlers discussed that it could be Tiger that had pulled them into the hat and looked devastated that they thought that they had lost the battle, and they were about to become Windowir's as well.

Miana could see what the bowlers' plan was to try to cure the trees by their scowling facial expressions!

Jay drew a snake with his pen.

Harry attempted to try to beg Miana to put the trees back onto earth.

Miana just got angry and was about to shoot the bowlers to turn them into Windowir's pointing her gun at them.

Jay's snake suddenly came alive, starting to attack Miana just in time before they were shot.

They all put their pen wigs on shooting at Miana.

A gang of Windowir's appeared out of nowhere.

Jake's snake started to attack the Windowir's, also distracting them.

Paul drew a large, smooth shield to protect them from the bullets.

Charlie spoke. "Do you know why the bullet lost its job?"

Ben replied. "Why did it lose its job?"

Charlie replied. "Because it got fired."

They laughed.

The Windowir's started shooting at the bowlers, with bullets bouncing back from the shield at themselves, killing themselves.

The bowlers shot groups of Windowir's with the wig bullets, one Windowir was left running away from the bowlers shooting random shots behind him.

The bowlers ran behind the Windowir dodging the bullets, they then grabbed the Windowir between them just before he had entered the bright doorway holding the Windowir down on the floor.

Darren drew a pair of handcuffs around the Windowir's wrists.

Jay drew a chair, they sat the Windowir down on the chair questioning the Windowir where the key to the book was hidden.

The Windowir refused to say anything.

Darren suddenly got so excited noticing a shiny key on a large poster full of flowers in the water on the wall with it saying Opack above it.

Jay commented. "It could be the key to fit the padlock, I hope!"

Robert looked disappointed. "Oh no, it was just a poster!"

The bowlers needed a way to get to Opack to save the trees and take them back down to earth.

A pair of hands came from above out of nowhere, grabbing Tom's legs and pulling him into the air making him vanish.

The bowlers pushed the blue talk button, asking Tom where he was.

Tom replied, saying that he had no idea where he was.

Cara stood close to the poster looking at it in more detail; the poster was full of red water and flowers surrounding a key that you could not see unless you were close up to it.

George and Ben looked closely also at the key on the poster, noticing that the key looked really camouflaged in the poster, making it hard to see for a reason they thought.

George picked the key out of the poster, feeling ecstatic to end evil, in the hope that the key would enter the padlock.

Penny looked at Eric in the hope that there was more good than bad to come with a bit of good luck happening.

Darker red water started to bubble and swirl around in the poster, the red water poured out of the poster, then travelled to their feet, then up their bodies, and they started to feel paralysed from the red water not being able to move.

The bowlers were crying hysterically and panicking, deciding what to do next, as the red water hit their chins, the Windowir was drowning as well.

Charlie managed to shout Zon just before his mouth was covered, drowning them to death.

Zon arrived with them in a flash, suddenly the red water fell to the floor from their bodies, and after a short while, they started to be un-paralysed with Zon vanishing again.

Jake made a point saying that this had been the warning of what was going to happen on the outside of the bubble earlier with the virtual gun and the red water coming out when they were surrounded by water.

The bowlers noticed that the Windowir had drowned feeling a little sad that another life had been taken away.

Darren and Jay drew their ink back into their pens.

Penny and Eric hugged, with everybody hugging them also happy to be alive.

George showed the rest of the team the key that he had found in the poster, all that they could see was a sea of trees in front of them.

One by one they all had hands grab them from above, throwing them into a room above, they were relieved to be back with Tom.

A large gang of Windowir's appeared in front of them from a bright doorway shooting at them.

The bowlers attempted to grab the guns from the Windowir's, with no success pushing their blue buttons on their pens, they then placed their wigs onto their heads and then pressed their yellow buttons to shoot the Windowir's with each hair bullet.

Robert noticed and pointed out that there was a blue button on the side of the key.

Charlie pressed the blue button on the key in the hope that it would help them.

Suddenly the key threw out a force field stopping the bullets from hitting them, and bouncing back at the Windowirs, only when the button was pressed, they found out that the force field lets bullets through it to hit the Windowirs.

27

George's memory Jar had a blue smiley face that lit up. Then it popped open.

Charlie's finger slid off the blue button by mistake on the key, with the bullets speeding towards them.

The bowlers dodged the bullets screaming in panic mode, cuddling Rex and Bruno to protect them.

A bullet made a deep scratch in Robert's leg while it scraped past him, making him limp away.

Darren's blue smiley face lit up, his bottle top popped off knocking a Windowir out cold on the floor, this distracted the rest of the Windowir's with the smell of cheesy feet and the green fog in the air stopping them from shooting because they could not see.

Charlie spoke. "I tried to catch the fog the other day, but I missed."

Jake laughed, with everyone else joining in.

Darren's blue smiley face went back to normal with the top shutting again.

Chris got his pen out of his pocket and drew his own oil gun, picking it up and shooting at the Windowir's.

Charlie's finger slid off the blue button on the key, stopping the force field from protecting them.

The Windowir's were oily and started to come around a little.

The bowlers pressed the top on their pens, releasing their wigs and then pressed their yellow buttons on their pens, squeezing them and shooting the Windowir's.

Some Windowir's were left alive.

Robert questioned the alive Windowir's why they needed to take people to turn them into Windowir's and take the trees from earth.

The Windowir's explained that they need the trees and people more than Earth to turn other planets similar to Earth, stealing their trees and turning people into Windowirs making it clear that earth is the first of many to be destroyed.

A tall, strange man with a tall large glass hat from earlier that pulled them into the hat appeared from behind the Windowir's with an evil look on his face, he had a hat full of bullets on his head introducing himself as Tiger pointing at his large pile of guns on the floor that he had stolen and turned them into needle bullet guns.

Jake blurted out saying. "So, it is you that has been causing trouble!"

Tiger replied. "Yes, and you are here with no way back out of Opack to get back to your planet Earth that will be ruined by us and yourselves very soon!"

The bowlers panicked, and said goodbye to each other, with Penny and Eric holding hands.

Tiger pulled his glass gun out of his pocket.

Tom suddenly drew a large toilet with his pen, pulling it out of the drawing.

The bowlers teamed up together, picking Tiger up and throwing him into the air; the bowlers had caught him, they then threw Tiger into the toilet headfirst, he was starting to drown gasping for air and fighting to get back out of the toilet.

The Windowir's were shooting at the bowlers.

The bowlers dodged the needle bullets.

George's jar had a lit-up blue smiley face, his memory jar opened up, releasing nothing.

The Windowir's suddenly changed their behaviour for the better.

George's blue smiley face on his jar went back to normal with it shutting, and it was still empty inside.

The bowlers could tell that the Windowir's were deep in thought, they were standing looking into the air like they were thinking about their previous lives before they became Windowir's dropping their guns to the floor.

Tiger pulled his head out of the toilet carrying on shouting at the bowlers that they would not open the book that he had padlocked, demanding that the bowlers will join the

Windowir's, and angrily asked for the key back that they had stolen from the poster.

A Windowir appeared from behind the dazed Windowir's who were in deep thought.

Jay pressed the top of his pen, releasing his wig; he pressed his yellow button, releasing his bullets and shooting at Tiger and the Windowir's.

The bowlers did not know what to do next, hoping that more Windowir's did not appear.

The key started to flash, pulling the group together like super glue squashing George in the middle.

The rings and the tattoo ring flashed white suddenly ejecting the bowlers, and some trees back down to earth in a large, very long translucent fluorescent light-yellow pipe while holding onto the key and putting their wigs back into their pens feeling happy to be on their way back down to planet earth, with them noticing that trees were flying up the opposite way to planet Opack.

Cara and Penny looked so concerned with an upset look on their faces about the green trees with roots attached continuing to enter planet Opack from the earth.

The rest of the bowlers could not wait to see if it was the correct key to fit into the padlock on the book, landing on the floor with a bump exiting the tube.

Harry insisted on a proud achievement selfie on his eye finger of them all touching the key travelling back to the bubble with them all smiling, pressing their black buttons, then blowing their whistles flying along most of the way struggling to look at the 3D map.

People looked up in shock at them flying along holding hands, with the loud strange noises coming from the whistles.

Penny suggested pressing the star on the 3D map after travelling halfway.

Cara thought that it would be a good idea to press the star to save them time asking the bowlers to touch the star, explaining that this way they would arrive at the bubble faster, as they touched the star on the 3D map they struggled to help Rex and Bruno to touch it with their paws, transporting them through time.

Penny noticed and pointed out first that the star on the map was burning hot to the touch, with them all having to take their fingers off fast.

They sat in the bubble with Rex and Bruno in the middle, with no sign of land and water all around them.

Chris suggested that Tiger must have made the 3D map button hot so that they would burn their fingers and let go and they hopefully would not use it again.

The bowlers were struggling to breathe and were starting to panic that they were stuck with not enough air to breathe surrounded by an ocean, suddenly a submarine appeared in front of the bubble attaching to the outside of the bubble, a glass translucent large door formed for them to enter the submarine, as they left the bubble they looked a little bit happier.

Robert noticed and pointed out that Philip was still encouraging sleepy Rex and Bruno out of the bubble behind them, noticing small boxes at the side of the walkway into the submarine saying press me on the side.

Ray could not resist the temptation of looking at the box and pressing the button on the box.

Suddenly the lid popped off, a pink flower appeared spewing out tiny dust from the middle of the flower all over the bowlers, the dust started to form into a person shape.

Harry drew a fine net with his pen, picking it up to catch the dust with no success, the dust person started to chase behind them.

Eric and Paul put their wigs on shooting at the dust, with no success with the bullets going straight through the dust.

Robert drew a hair dryer to blow the dust person away, the dust put itself back together, still chasing behind them.

They looked exhausted from running out of breath.

28

The fire started to chase them, it left smouldering marks on their clothes.

Paul shouted Zon out loud.

Zon arrived, then blew the dust into the air, giving them the chance to run.

Paul shouted thank you to Zon, he said you're welcome with a smile, then went again, disappearing in a blink.

There was a door in front of them saying safety on it, they entered inside of the door, shutting the door behind them.

They felt sorry for Rex and Bruno getting dragged about.

There was a large roaring cosy fire in a large fireplace inside of the room, they were standing in front of the fire getting cosy, the fire suddenly started to chase them causing smouldering burn marks on their clothes, they felt like they were on the bridge in the newspaper clipping from earlier.

Philip thought and announced that he thought that was the end of them all.

Jake and Charlie started screaming, with the fire about to touch them.

Chris removed his magical shower hat from his whistle putting his hat on the correct way using it to turn into a large ice-cold snowball, with the rest of the bowlers following his lead, they stood melting fast with Cara, Philip, Ray and Penny in the middle of them protecting them.

Ray suggested. "Another option is to go and ask Leo for his advice!"

Darren drew a crisp bag in front of him, throwing the crisp bag onto the floor in the middle of them.

Charlie spoke. "I have just created a totally new flavour of crisp, if it is successful, I will make a packet."

Robert replied. "I like that joke."

Chris pressed the silver button on the petal, turning it into a tattoo bag again holding hands, and tails then used the tattoo bag to enter into the floor through the crisp bag to ask for advice from Leo on what they should do next.

Leo praised the bowlers with a smile, saying that the main thing was that they have the key, suggesting for them to have a rest and then carry on when someone had thought of something.

The bowlers were very happy to be there.

Robert noticed the alcoholic drink Qui picking it up, pouring them all a drink, they had a few drinks of Qui each while brainstorming what to do next.

Leo suggested that if they were to touch their body with the rings that they were wearing on their fingers, it would heal themselves in hope.

They all touched their saw areas on their bodies with their rings, healing them in shock that they felt well with no pain again.

Harry got everybody to touch his eye finger on the last photo that he had taken, and they immediately got transported back to just before they had set off back to the bubble and travelled back in the bubble to the shipwreck.

Chris touched the silver button on the bag, turning it back into a petal.

The bowlers arrived, walking into the shipwreck.

Tom put the key into the lock with the book opening, they looked shocked that they had finally opened the book, inside of the book was a large bottle saying virus cure.

Jake picked the virus cure bottle out of the book, looking puzzled, not knowing what to do with it, commenting and panicking that there would be nowhere near enough virus cure to go around and cure everybody.

The bowlers travelled back in the bubble, then they left the bubble with the virus cure still safe in Jake's hands.

A large group of Windowir's were stood trying to grab the virus cure out of Jake's hands.

Darren started to draw a large wall.

The rest of the bowlers joined in between shooting, and fighting the Windowir's, they sheltered behind the wall using their pen wigs to shoot at the Windowir's.

The Windowir's started to shoot back at the bowlers.

A Windowir knocked the virus cure bottle from Jake's hands making some spill to the floor under a tree, the tree immediately grew extra leaves on it, with some falling off onto the Windowir's, the Windowir's that got touched by the leaves, all of a sudden, they looked confused asking where they were.

A sudden gale-force wind started to blow out of nowhere.

Some leaves from the tree that the virus cure touched blew on, touching other ground and trees nearby, the trees immediately started to grow back, curing more Windowir's back to normal people with the leaves touching them.

Darren commented. "I am so shocked at how strange it is, with leaves falling from the trees, with it nearly being May and the leaves don't normally fall from the trees in May!"

The rest agreed with Darren watching them fall to the floor.

Cara and Darren started to put a few of the leaves that had cured people into their pockets, with the others doing the same in case they needed them later, they travelled to different cities sprinkling the virus cure, and leaves from their pockets near to the dying trees, there were only a few precious drops of virus cure left in the bottle.

Their next problem was Tiger, the Windowir's and Vord on planet Opack.

As they were walking along, they noticed dead Windowir's coming back to life following behind them that had been touched by healthy leaves, they touched the star on the map together travelling up to Opack, on the way up Jay joked that older Robert may be up there with him disappearing.

Darren spoke. "I doubt it."

As they arrived at Opack, some Windowir's were shooting at them, one shot the jar of virus cure with it exploding onto the floor a little bit too far away from the infected trees, and they released their pen wig guns shooting back at the Windowir's.

Jay noticed and pointed out older Robert from a distance, pointing him out to the rest of the bowlers.

Older Robert started to join in with the Windowir's shooting at the bowlers.

<u>29</u>

<u>Robert removed the paper from the envelope in his pocket. Snowballs?</u>

The bowlers looked extremely shocked to see older Robert trying to talk with him, with him pointing his gun at them, he was just interested in shooting them.

Their rings suddenly lit up orange, and blue with a mixed flashing pattern.

George commented just as he got shot with him thinking that it must be

Zon attempting to help them with the rings lighting up.

Charlie touched a Windowir with his ring by mistake.

Robert pointed out that the Windowir that had been touched by Charlie's ring had stopped shooting at them.

Darren knew from the back of his thoughts that the rings were another way to turn the Windowir's back to normal, explaining to everybody his thoughts.

Charlie spoke. "Do you know which planet is the richest?"

Jake replied. "What is the answer?"

Charlie replied. "Saturn, because it has got so many precious rings!"

Robert laughed, setting everyone off.

A tall shadow of a person from a distance with a large hat appeared, the person did not look very happy with Dragon Vord at the side of him.

Chris pointed out that it must be Tiger, with his dragon Vord at the side of him walking towards them appearing next to the bowlers.

The people that used to be Windowir's started to follow the bowlers, Vord started to breathe fire, burning them all, and the bowlers could not get close enough to touch Tiger and Vord with their rings.

Paul drew snowballs in the air with his pen, he was then able to pick them up, they were as cold as ice throwing them at Vord, the other bowlers joined in, but no matter how fast they threw the snowballs at Tiger and Vord they melted immediately with the heat from the flames out of Vord's mouth.

Robert drew a bucket of water, he was able to pick it up and throw it over Tiger and Vord hoping to stop the flames from hitting them, people who used to be Windowir's had taken a step away to save themselves.

Paul opened his pocket watch with the loud concert noise distracting Tiger and Vord.

The bowlers drew as many snowballs as they could between them.

Jake took the lead, running up to Tiger and Vord with their hands full of snowballs, attempting to avoid the flames while shooting at the same time with their wigs, the bowlers touched Tiger and Vord with their orange and blue rings.

The rings made a little difference, because Vord had stopped breathing fire and started to chase them, and Tiger just stood and laughed watching them, they drew the ink back into their pens, and the bowlers and ex Windowir's ran away as fast as they could.

Older Robert was walking towards them, looking a little dazed with a leaf on his head.

Rex and Bruno growled at Tiger and Vord loudly.

Robert noticed some drips of virus cure trickling near to some trees, he pointed it out to the rest of the bowlers and suddenly leaves on the trees started to fall, hitting Tiger and Vord.

Vord suddenly stopped chasing them, and Tiger had an evil look, but he then suddenly looked a little bit happier.

Harry drew an oil coin pouring the oil all over the pair, the pair looked blank in the face, and calmer.

Cara commented that they must be confused because they have probably always been evil.

Robert removed the paper from the envelope in his pocket; he looked at it, putting it onto the floor in front of him, not sure why they had it.

Harry drew the ink back into his pen.

Philip picked up the blank paper from the floor that had come from the envelope and touched Vord, and Tiger with the paper.

Suddenly Tiger and Vord's personalities had changed, asking if they were home on Opack and questioning who the bowlers were in a calm manner like they had swallowed a chill out-pill.

Older Robert stood with them, asking where he was.

They explained that he was shot but was going home.

The bowlers questioned Tiger why he would do these things.

Tiger replied, saying that Opack was a better place with him and his Windowir's in charge.

The bowlers disagreed and explained that Tiger and Vord needed to help to heal planet Earth.

Tiger explained that the virus cure was probably one of the last bottles stolen from him.

The bowlers asked what he meant.

Tiger explained that a lady had stolen the virus cure bottles one at a time from him and that she had hidden the bottles away from Tiger so that he could not move as many trees from Earth, he could only carry on curing the trees with the virus cure when they had got to Opack.

The bowlers understood that Tiger could not move any more trees without the cure, and asked how they only cured a tree at a time without curing the Windowir's?

Tiger explained that the Windowir's were told not to go near any leaves and if any Windowir changed back to normal, they were shot and turned back into Windowir's.

The bowlers were curious who this lady was, saying that there were probably many more bottles of virus cure out there, and it could be the same lady that had passed the 3D map, and the rings onto them.

Tiger explained that it does not matter because they have got the planet Earth to mend, the leaves eventually cured all of the world, with the leaves travelling on people's shoes, cars, and planes, etc.

Tiger and Vord started to help to get Earth back to normal by spreading more of the healing leaves around different places.

The bowlers touched any remaining burns on their bodies with their rings that they had missed, curing themselves better.

Paul drew a crisp bag on the floor.

Chris pressed the silver button, turning it back to the tattoo bag.

The bowlers insisted that Tiger and Vord needed to go with them to see Leo so that they could show Leo their excellent outcome results.

The bowlers used the tattoo bag holding hands and re-entered the crisp bag.

Leo was sitting looking up at them in shock, frightened for his life, with him looking like he was going to cry.

The bowlers told Leo not to worry, explaining that they had changed them so much for the better with the evil eliminated.

Leo then had a big smile on his face.

Tiger and Vord helped Leo as well as others with future problems around the earth.

The guns on Opack worried Leo a little in case they got into the wrong hands again, and he explained that he would lock the guns up at some point.

The bowlers pointed at the crisp bag at the roof re-entering earth, leaving Tiger, and Vord with Leo.

Robert pressed the silver button on the bag, turning it back into a silver petal and put it into his pocket.

Tom commented that they should call their adventure the world of present, future, and past with them travelling through time.

The bowlers agreed.

Penny and Eric did not want to part.

Eric said that he would walk and fly down to see her often, explaining that Penny needed to live her life in twenty-twenty-four, with the ring still tattooed on her finger.

Penny agreed, going back to her life if she knew where Eric lived.

They all went to Eric's house to just look at it from a distance to show Penny where he lived.

Eric promised that he would travel to meet up with her, and they flew Penny home to twenty-twenty-four.

They were then transported back to twenty-seventy-five, then they flew older Robert, Cara, Ray, and Philip back to older Paul's house and talked about what had happened on their journey, and the excellent results.

Charlie wanted to stop at the super value shop, opening his pocket watch releasing all of the money, with the shopkeeper looking shocked, with him saying buy the shop if you wish.

Charlie laughed and then purchased three extra large hot tubs from the super value shop.

The bowlers then travelled back to older Paul's house and had a party before they left with loud music playing sat in the hot tubs together drinking Blue Rock Cool, they hugged each other saying bye for now, and then the bowlers re-entered back into twenty-twenty-five through their whistles, hoping for another adventure in the near future, with the time zone the same as they had left their last adventure, as they arrived Penny was sitting outside Eric's house.

The End.

About the author

Anita Kirk is from Yorkshire in the United Kingdom, she works full time and writes many book genres in her spare time with unlimited talent to write anything, she loves swimming, line dancing, holidays, music, films, writing, reading and spending time with friends and family.

All of Anita Kirk's books have got <u>funny moments </u>that may make you feel like laughing your socks off.

In a Quarter of a second and the Glowing Rings has got two magical action-packed time travel adventures inside.

Dream Changing is about a lady who can see people's dreams and can change them.
Does Flora help to save the world after

visiting the opticians
receiving more hassle
and drama than she
bargained for?

Sexy Antics is for adults to
enjoy, you will never
look at a magazine in the
same way again.

Magical Footsteps has got a
friend that has gone
missing that needs
finding with help from
strangers, with them

ending up inside of a
game.

 Unexpected Jewel has got
different stories inside
full of mythical
creatures, and it is full of
magic.

Sexy Shenanigans has got
four stories for adults to
enjoy with the last story
having horror inside as
well.

Christmas Sparkles has got fairies inside of this book and a fairytale cottage where they live, the fairies need help from two children and other people to get people onto the nice list to save Christmas, with so much more inside for you to enjoy.

Mel's Adventure has got a story with pictures for

the younger end or anyone that needs a simple story to learn the alphabet, with a song and a few words in a different language to learn as well.

<u>The Sound of Ticking</u> is about a man who owns a shop in New York and receives a telescope for his birthday, his life is soon turned upside down with unpredictable challenging situations taking him to many places in time to solve many mysteries.

Wings to Heaven. This is a true story about my dad's life before, during and after dementia and Alzheimer's.

Sexy Revenge is for adults only, it's about a man that has a car accident, and his life is stolen by his best friend while he's in a coma, does Jenson kick some ass getting his own back?

__TIME TRAVEL LIP BALM__
Enjoy the adventure, the lip balm dramas inside of this book are very unpredictable and fun, it's full of jokes and lighthearted entertainment for anyone to enjoy from adults to children.

<u>Fun Dance Book One</u> has got many dances to follow by yourself or with others, it is ideal for any age.

<u>Spooky Scary</u> needs garlic circles and so much more to bring people back to normal everyday life with many obstacles and drama along the way.

These books have been written so far with many more available soon.

Remember that you can follow and contact Anita Kirk with any questions or comments on Tick Tock, Facebook, Twitter, LinkedIn or you can email any comments to anitajane1@outlook.com Please contact Anita if you would like a shop opening or anything else and she will get back to

you as soon as possible
with an answer.
If you have enjoyed reading
Anita Kirk's books a
good review would be
appreciated and if you
could share Anita's
books on your social
media, and with your
family and friends she
would really appreciate
your help.
Thank you for your
support in reading
this book.
All of Anita Kirk's books
are available on

Amazon and some other online shops.

A good review would mean a lot if you have enjoyed this book.
Thank you in advance for your good positive review it is very much appreciated.

Thank you again